KT-556-530

Murder, Mystery and Mayhem is Jennifer Carnell's first novel, written when she was only sixteen years of age. She is currently attending sixth form college in her home town of Hastings in East Sussex, where she is studying English Literature, History and Sociology.

Murder, Mystery and Mayhem

JENNIFER CARNELL

FONTANA/Collins

First published by William Collins 1988
First issued in Fontana Paperbacks 1989

Copyright © Jennifer Carnell 1988

Decorative initials by Oriol Bath

Made and printed in Great Britain by
William Collins Sons & Co. Ltd, Glasgow

To my mother and father
with all my love

Chapter One

iss Fry had left Penton. The villagers were amazed and Miss Fry's departure was destined to become the most popular subject of gossip for many months. Very little happened in the small village of Penton, so naturally this was big news. Some people said that they had been expecting something of this nature to happen but the majority were surprised.

The previous month, November, Miss Fry's elderly tyrannical father had died. He had been taking his dog for a walk on the nearby cliff top on a particularly windy day when he had suddenly fallen over the edge, taking the dog with him. Miss Fry had just completed a course in taxidermy at the local college and had been delighted to receive a prize for progress at the end of term, but immediately after the tragedy she had looked so heartbroken that everyone had felt sorry for her. All the same, everyone admired how quickly she had pulled herself together sufficiently to organize the funeral arrangements.

The Women's Institute, who spent their weekly coffee mornings on gossip rather than flower arranging, noted that Miss Fry seemed to be in unusually high spirits after the funeral was over. Certainly she had reason to be happy

– she had, after all, been the sole beneficiary from the will – but her outlook on life seemed to have been slightly modified.

Miss Fry was a spinster of about sixty-five who had spent most of her life attending to her father's every want and whim. She had always had a reputation for being prudent, or perhaps just plain stingy, but since her father's passing on there had been several uncharacteristic extravagances. One day Miss Fry had been observed, through her neighbour's net curtains, leaving Penton on her ancient bicycle and returning with a second-hand Rolls-Royce. Very few people, apart from the Colonel, the vicar and Mr Winifred Jones owned cars so Miss Fry's rather erratic driving came as an unpleasant shock. During the following weeks the newly mobile Miss Fry's driving skill did not improve. There had been at least six proven accidents attributed to her, a damaged hedge, two broken gates ('I didn't even see them'), two smashed walls ('ridiculous place to have a wall'), and she had also knocked Constable Blockett off his bicycle ('It was his own fault – in this day and age there shouldn't be bicycles on the road, cars are the only way to travel'). It was just as well that there were very few cars in Penton as any motorist's or pedestrian's life was in considerable danger when Miss Fry was around. After Mrs Barton, the head of the Women's Institute, was nearly flattened on her way to a meeting, she and the other women decided that it was their civic duty to start a petition to remove Miss Fry from the road. They spent the rest of the day canvassing support, but on the following morning when they went to Miss Fry's cottage to present her with the lengthy petition, they found to their trepidation that Miss Fry and her car had left Penton, apparently for good.

The Women's Institute were naturally angry and, at first, stunned. To them it seemed inconsiderate of Miss

Fry to vanish just as they had managed to persuade the editor of the local newspaper to run a series of articles on the dangers of motorists. When the women had recovered from the shock their tongues swept into full production over the very curious disappearance of Miss Fry. Their immediate reaction was that one of their members had done the unspeakable, turned traitor and warned Miss Fry to leave the village before Mrs Barton and her retinue arrived at the cottage. This was not as unlikely as it sounds. It was well known by non-members that being questioned by the women was not unlike an interrogation by the Spanish Inquisition. Two years ago, when rumours had circulated about the vicar's relationship with his cleaning woman, the Women's Institute had looked upon it as their duty to find out the truth. So, one Sunday morning after the service, they had invited themselves to the vicarage for tea and cakes. No one outside the group ever found out what the 'truth' was, but the gardener, who had been watching through the French windows as he pruned the roses, had later sworn that he had seen tears running freely down the vicar's rosy cheeks and dropping into his cup of tea.

This story was borne out by Emily Bennet, an ex-member of the Institute who had, some time before, been forced to resign by the other elite members because she had refused to reveal her exact relationship with the Colonel, with whom she had tea and cherry buns every Saturday. She said that she had seen the dreaded Women's Institute departing from the vicarage looking smugly triumphant. They had then marched further down the street, knocked on the unfortunate cleaning woman's door and invited themselves inside the house for tea and ginger-bread. It was fair to assume that the cleaning woman – she was called Zambini, which was unfortunate in itself – had been subjected to a lengthy lecture on morality,

since the only contact between Zambini and the vicar that
followed was a weekly handshake after Sunday morning
service. That could hardly be deemed scandalous since
the vicar gave a handshake to everybody. It was reported
by the vicar's butler at the local pub, the 'Lonesome
Heart', that he was being made to do all the household
cleaning at the vicarage since the vicar seemed extremely
reluctant to employ a replacement for Zambini. It appeared that the vicar was determined to avoid any further
gossip, since the next cleaning woman was nearly ninety
years old, and her breath smelt strongly of the humbugs
that she was always sucking – consequently the few teeth
that she did have were black. The new cleaning woman,
who was called Rosie, liked to call herself a 'charwoman',
and not even the Women's Institute was able to speculate
or insinuate relations of any kind between her and the
vicar.

After the initial shock of Miss Fry's sudden departure
the women naturally wanted to find out why she had gone
and where exactly she had gone to. Research was quickly
undertaken and the gossips pooled their knowledge of
Miss Fry's movements over the last few months. The first
thing to find out was the whereabouts of Harold Fry.
Harold was a goldfish, Miss Fry's goldfish. It was generally
thought that Miss Fry would have taken Harold with her
since he was her only companion now that her father was
dead. It came as a surprise to find that the goldfish was
now living with the vicar, who told them that he had been
asked by Miss Fry to be custodian of Harold and to keep
him in the manner to which he was accustomed.

The verdict was suicide! To the Women's Institute it
seemed obvious that Miss Fry must have been lamenting
the death of her father and that she had fallen into a fit of
suicidal depression. It was as clear as a blue sky to Mrs
Hellsworthy; she said that Miss Fry had given her only

friend to a good home, got in her car and driven off the top of the very same cliff that her late father had fallen from. This theory became the general consensus of the group and all agreed that it was only a matter of time before the bloody remains of Miss Fry were discovered.

Mrs Dorton suggested nervously that perhaps Miss Fry had gone to France again. She was cried down immediately; this did not conform to their nice little suicide. There had never been a suicide in the village of Penton so naturally they were anxious to have one. Another of the uncharacteristic things that Miss Fry had done since her father's death had been to go to France for a week. This, for a spinster of sixty-five whose idea of a holiday abroad should have been to go to Bournemouth, had been quite revolutionary. Miss Fry had made no secret of her departure and, being a highly organized person who did not make her mind up at a moment's notice, had planned who was to accommodate Harold and written letters to cancel all deliveries of milk, newspapers and fish food, several weeks in advance. The Women's Institute had been very much intrigued at Miss Fry's first venture into the outside world, and had wondered what could have caused such a curious thing to happen. Various explanations had been offered, the most popular being either that Miss Fry was hoping to find an eligible millionaire in Paris to marry, or that she was a secret drinker who had decided to experiment with French wines. None of these rumours had been taken up in earnest, partly because Miss Fry had always maintained a prim exterior and was therefore unlikely to be either an alcoholic or a gold digger, and partly because at the time the Women's Institute had been too busy organizing various charitable events to raise money for 'teaching little children in India how to become good Christians'. Being very narrow-minded they knew nothing of poverty in England but considered it good and dutiful to contribute money to a charitable organization – that was probably bogus – to help a far-flung part of the Empire. It was all very nice to raise money for little children in India, but had one turned up at their front door it would probably have been hit over the head with the nearest vase and reprimanded for impudence.

Miss Fry had returned from France in high spirits. She had spent the week in Paris seeing all the sights. When Mrs Barton had asked her if she had made the acquaintance of any eligible millionaires the surprised reply had been not as far as she knew. Nor had there been any sign of bottles of wine, but instead Miss Fry had brought home with her several large cheeses, none of which anyone had seen her eat, and none of which had been given away.

To Mrs Barton, suicide seemed to be the foregone conclusion to Miss Fry's life. She said proudly that her brother-in-law's cousin had ended it all by placing his head in a gas oven. So she knew all there was to know about suicide, or so she claimed, and she said that Miss Fry had had the very same look in her eyes as her brother-in-law's cousin. This to the Women's Institute proved everything.

Before the tragic death of Miss Fry's father, visitors had been quite frequent at Honeycombe Cottage. Mr Fry liked to flatter himself by having ladies at the cottage for tea and hot cross buns, so members of the Institute had often invited themselves to tea. Mr Fry had always extracted great enjoyment from telling them about the time he had been presented to Queen Victoria, so the visits could be very dreary, but the hot cross buns were exceptionally good and more than compensated for the boredom. Miss Fry's mother had died when Miss Fry was a young debutante and Miss Fry had ended up looking after her father. She had taken over the duties of her late mother, the most important of which had been to make thirty hot cross buns every week. Miss Fry had led a fairly staid life with only occasional excitements such as showing her pet goldfish at the local pet show; her crowning glory had been when she had won a small cup for Harold and got her picture in the local paper. After her father's death there had been no more tea parties and hot cross buns. Indeed Miss Fry had had no one inside the cottage, so suspicion arose that perhaps Mr Fry's antique fishing-rod collection had been sold.

Miss Fry's suicide had come at a good time for the Institute since for the past few weeks they had been longing to get inside Honeycombe Cottage in order to have a good snoop round. So having recovered from the disappointment of being unable to give the car petition to Miss Fry, they decided that this was the perfect opportunity to go inside the cottage. Mrs Barton ordered her husband to stop working in their vegetable patch and to get his tool kit. In no time at all, Mr Barton had the front door off its hinges and the ladies were free to explore. All the furniture was left intact and the fishing-rod collection was in the usual position, hanging on the wall in the kitchen. However most of Miss Fry's personal possessions were gone. The clothes were gone from the wardrobe; the hairbrush, comb, perfume and other such things no longer lay on the dressing table. It appeared that the essentials had gone rather than items of value. There were two explanations available to the ladies: either Miss Fry, being the sentimental type, had driven off the cliff accompanied by suitcases full of clothes, or she was not smashed to smithereens after all.

The women sat pondering in the small drawing room, when their explanation arrived, or at least part of it. A Mr and Mrs Hamilton appeared, a little bemused to find the front door of their new cottage lying on the front lawn.

It soon became clear that Miss Fry was not dead but had simply sold her home lock, stock and barrel.

But where was Miss Fry?

Chapter Two

iss Fry drove merrily along the winding country road, singing as she went. It was the thirtieth of December and although the sun was shining the air was very chilly. The cold did not dampen Miss Fry's high spirits because she had her thermal underwear to keep her warm.

She was a small woman with short curly grey hair, green eyes and silver-framed round spectacles. She wore a tartan kilt, a white frilly blouse, an angora-wool sweater, beige coat, heavy black shoes, a tartan scarf and beret. For the first time in her sixty-five years Miss Fry felt free. She had often wondered how it would feel to be able to do precisely what she wanted and now she was going to find out. Of course she was going to miss Harold and she did feel a little guilty at having left him at the vicarage; but the vicar had always been good with goldfish so he would be happy – and a car was no place for Harold.

For many years Miss Fry had speculated as to what she would be able to do should her father die and she had on occasions wished that he would hurry up and do it. Mr Fry seemed to have super-human strength, living to ninety-five, and he remained bad tempered and bossy right until the tragic end. When this came Miss Fry had of course been delighted, and had found it difficult to maintain a suitable exterior of mourning and sobriety. This was understandable in the circumstances: she was no longer young herself, and she had begun to wonder if perhaps her father was going to outlive her . . .

She had sold Honeycombe Cottage, complete with furniture and fishing rods, relatively cheaply in order to sell it quickly. She had only bidden farewell to one person in the village and that had been the vicar. Miss Fry was glad to leave Penton. She had few, if any friends, and her brief liaisons with the butcher and the Colonel had been effectively terminated by Mr Fry. She had disliked the gossipy ways of the Women's Institute and the way the group undermined all the non-members' reputations. The only rules and regulations in Penton were drawn up and supervised by the Institute, so the village was all but in name ruled by these busybodies.

The Fry family originated from Spain but had come to England during the 1750s as performers in a circus. The Fry family had settled in England and the descendants of the gypsy circus performers had become as English as tea at four o'clock, or croquet on the vicar's lawn on a Sunday afternoon. They were deeply ashamed of their ancestors and so pretended to their friends that they came from a long line of English gentlemen. Their humble origins were only discussed in hushed whispers behind closed doors and when the children were safely tucked up in bed. Mr Fry, being a responsible parent, had kept the dark secrets of the Fry family away from his daughter as he knew that such knowledge could so easily destroy her confidence; if she mentioned it to anyone her whole social status would be ruined. So Mr Fry died happy, believing that the past history of the Frys had died too.

Miss Fry, however, knew the terrible truth. When Mr

Fry had married Mrs Fry he had neglected to tell his wife about the gypsy connections. This was quite natural since that information alone provided grounds strong enough for her to reject his proposal. What Mr Fry had not bargained for was the inquisitiveness of his new wife. He knew very little about the nature of women, so he did not know that the only way to keep something secret from his wife was to lock it in a chest and sink it in the middle of the ocean. The young bride soon tired of sweeping the kitchen while her husband was at work and it was only a matter of days before she ventured into the cellar of Honeycombe Cottage.

The cellar was dark and gloomy and possibly haunted. Mrs Fry climbed down the wooden ladder which was damp and rotten; a candle was her only light. Apart from six bottles of blackberry wine the only thing in the cellar was a large wooden crate. The crate had writing in red paint on the side. The words were in Spanish, which she could not read, but there was no mistaking them: 'Señor Carlos Fry, Señora Carmen Fry'. With trembling hands Mrs Fry opened up the crate. Inside were several bundles of brightly coloured clothes made out of silk, satin and velvet. At first she feared that the crate had belonged to pirate members of the family, but she soon found the naked truth to be far worse. At the bottom of the crate was a large portfolio of circus programmes, posters and newspaper cuttings. With a heavy and broken heart Mrs Fry left the cellar and went into the kitchen to await her husband's return from his office. As soon as Mr Fry walked through the front door she delivered her accusations. At first he denied all knowledge of a crate in the cellar, but after a few heavy blows from a rolling pin he admitted having married her under the false pretence of having come from a long line of English timber merchants. Mrs Fry, now that she knew the whole story, most certainly did not want any children. To her it seemed to be cruel and heartless to bring a poor innocent child into a family with such a dark, hideous past. However before she knew where she was, Mrs Fry found herself to be the mother of a little girl.

Mr Fry burnt the crate of incriminating evidence and scattered the ashes outside the Spanish Embassy in London. He had given strict orders to his wife that the family's past was to be kept from their daughter at all costs. Mrs Fry thought that her little Esmerelda had every right to know. It was hoped that their daughter would marry into high society and to Mrs Fry it seemed to be essential for Esmerelda to be told, to ensure that her future husband never had the chance to find out. So before her untimely death from influenza, Mrs Fry revealed the knowledge to her daughter with the strict orders that she should never tell her father that she knew. The information did not have the desired effect; Mrs Fry had expected her daughter to faint, at the least. Esmerelda thought that it was most exciting to have such common people as ancestors. She did not however know the whole story, nor had her mother. Señor Carlos Fry had been hanged as a compulsive murderer and thief.

Perhaps it was the gypsy blood in her that had suddenly made Miss Fry get up and leave Penton with no home to go to. It had not been completely impulsive however, as Miss Fry had known for over twenty years where she would go as soon as her father died. She had once read an article about a place called Waddington Castle. The castle belonged to Sir Horace Hedgeworthy, but he rarely lived there as he was stationed as an ambassador in the Bahamas. The castle was not opened for public display but instead was used as a very exclusive hotel for the aristocracy and wealthy Americans. Miss Fry had always been fascinated by such places and had decided to spend some of her savings on a short holiday at the castle. She was looking forward to meeting the other guests and seeing in the new year of 1937 in their company.

The history of the castle attracted her as much as anything else. She loved anything that was old, apart from her father, and had read several hundred historical romances in the last couple of years. Her father had not approved of her reading books of such a frivolous nature so Miss Fry had been forced to hide them under her bed; she had been unable to get the collection of 313 novels in the car so she had left them there. She wondered idly if Mr and Mrs Hamilton would read them, but she doubted it since the middle-aged couple had seemed interested only in joining the local fox hunt. Miss Fry had three new historical romances to read and she could hardly wait to start. One of them was by Daisy du Mariner, who was Miss Fry's favourite author. It was entitled *The Hangman and the Nursemaid*. According to the dust jacket it was about a nanny who looked after a little boy who grew up to be the local executioner. The nanny was jilted by her lover whom she accidentally killed. On being sentenced to death the hangman turned out to be her former ward. The story ended happily with them both running away to live a life of sin in the nearby mountains. This was just Miss Fry's cup of tea, and she hoped that it was suitably sad and heart-rending, as she always enjoyed a good cry.

Luckily the roads were not very busy. The Sussex roads were narrow and wound round bends very sharply. If a vehicle came along in the other direction Miss Fry tended to panic and her Rolls-Royce would swerve in a most dangerous fashion. The countryside was beautiful, perhaps too beautiful since Miss Fry's eyes were usually on the scenery rather than the speedometer or the road.

Miss Fry drove into the village of Waddington. It was much larger than Penton; it was in fact more of a town.

It had an impersonal feel to it, and was obviously the sort of place where everybody minded their own business. There were a good many people bustling around doing their shopping. In Penton, the arrival of someone in a Rolls-Royce would have made everyone stop, stare and gossip, but no one in Waddington appeared even remotely interested. 'It's amazing the difference twenty miles makes,' Miss Fry said to herself with wonder.

A little boy ran across the road and a very annoyed Miss Fry sounded the horn loudly at him. The little boy made a face and ran on. 'What a pity the days are over when children of that age were usefully occupied. I'm sure that angel-faced little horror would have made a splendid chimney sweep,' Miss Fry commented to herself.

Waddington Castle was not in the centre of the village but two miles outside. Miss Fry was exceeding the speed limit, though she was not aware of it, and she was in a hurry to get to her destination. 'I'm nearly there, I'm nearly there,' her mind chanted. She put her foot down and the car sped along even faster.

Looming in the distance at the top of a winding hill was Waddington Castle. It looked large and very impressive. Although it was called a castle it was in fact really a fortified mansion built on a hill, but castle sounded far grander in the travel brochures. Miss Fry drove past the gatehouse and up the castle driveway. On either side were lawns with peacocks strutting freely around. A pheasant ran across the road. Miss Fry, who did not care if the unfortunate bird could understand or not, yelled 'Get out of the way you obnoxious creature.'

Ordinarily Miss Fry was a polite, well-spoken lady who would be near to fainting if anyone used vulgar language, but when behind the wheel of a car she was like a demon possessed. She became totally unhinged from the little Miss Fry who was so respected and respectful. When

Constable Blockett had been knocked off his bicycle, Miss Fry had shouted various obscenities at the poor policeman, some of which he had only read in books.

Miss Fry parked the Rolls-Royce in a corner of the courtyard and looked around her to try and determine which of the many doors in view was the main entrance. A young man of about nineteen came out of the largest door and walked briskly across the courtyard to Miss Fry. He was wearing a porter's uniform, so it was safe for Miss Fry to assume that he was the castle's porter.

'Are you the porter, young man?' she asked, seeing no harm in checking.

'That's right, madam,' the porter said politely. His nose was bright red and he kept sniffing.

'Miss,' Miss Fry corrected. 'Miss Fry.'

'Can I help you . . . Miss Fry?' the porter asked patiently, wishing that Miss Fry would be a little quicker. His voice sounded a little hoarse and after he had sniffed for the umpteenth time he wiped his nose on the back of his hand.

'Hum . . .' murmured Miss Fry. She looked at the young man distastefully. She had been just about to shake his hand, but now changed her mind.

'Miss?' questioned the porter. He was used to dealing with vacant, slightly senile old ladies, and as far as he could see this was just another one.

'Perhaps you could carry my suitcases for me, my good man,' Miss Fry instructed. 'There are far too many to carry at one go, so perhaps you should take two now, show me my room and then come back for the rest.'

'Certainly, Miss Fry,' said the porter. He took the top two suitcases from the boot of the car and led the way across the courtyard and through the main entrance. 'Oh, this is wonderful, quite wonderful!' Miss Fry exclaimed enthusiastically.

The porter stared at her with curiosity as he thought to himself, 'Nutty as a fruitcake!'

The reception hall was like that of any large hotel. The carpet was a plush red, the lighting subdued and the furniture made from dark highly polished wood. The porter put the cases down on the floor while he waited for Miss Fry to sign the guest book at the desk.

'Miss Esmerelda Fry,' she said loudly and clearly, pronouncing every syllable with precision. The woman behind the desk, although young, was cold and stern. She gave Miss Fry an unfriendly stare.

'Would you care to sign our book?' she asked.

'What book?' asked Miss Fry, confused.

'The visitors' book,' the woman said, sounding mildly sarcastic. She raised her eyes to the ceiling trying to maintain a polite manner. 'So that we have a clear record of who is here and when,' she explained.

'Oh I see,' said Miss Fry. 'How very curious.' She had never had to do this at Bournemouth or at the little Paris hotel in the suburbs. She signed the leather-bound book with her small neat signature.

'David will show you to your room,' the woman said, nodding towards the porter who was coughing violently. 'If you need anything you can telephone directly here to the reception desk.'

'Thank you,' said Miss Fry. 'Please could I have my key?'

'We don't have room keys,' the receptionist replied coldly. 'They have never been necessary and there has never been a demand for them.'

'Oh I see,' Miss Fry said again, feeling very foolish. She followed the porter down a gloomy passageway that was lit only by oil lamps standing on each of the windowsills. The walls were oak panelled and hung with several oil paintings and prints. At length they came to a grand staircase that had a deep-blue carpet. Miss Fry felt overawed by the grandeur; this was certainly much more attractive than the little hotel in Bournemouth. The porter led her up the stairs and then through a door and down another passageway to a landing. Miss Fry noticed a second, less grand, flight of steps that led off from the landing, and paused for a moment, looking up with characteristic nosiness. From early childhood she had always had a reputation for inquisitiveness that had often made her unpopular at school. What had caught Miss Fry's attention was a pair of axes mounted on the wall about ten steps up.

'Are you coming, Miss Fry?' asked the porter impatiently. He was hungry and wanted a hot muffin from the kitchen. He also wanted to tell the other staff all about the new guest.

'Yes, I'm coming,' said Miss Fry with a sweet smile. 'I just got distracted for a moment.'

The porter opened the third door along the corridor which led off from the landing and ushered Miss Fry into a bedroom. 'I'll go and get the rest of your luggage, Miss Fry,' the porter said as he put the two suitcases down on the floor.

As soon as he had left, Miss Fry went over to the lead-mullioned French windows. She opened them and stepped out on to a balcony. She shut them behind her and leant over the balcony-rail to look at the view. It was not as spectacular as she had expected. She had a good view of half the roof of an opposite wing of the castle, and she could also see half the courtyard. She watched anxiously as the porter got the remaining luggage from the Rolls-Royce. She prayed that he would not drop the largest case as it contained something which was very precious and without which she could not manage. It was decidedly chilly, the sky was very white and Miss Fry suspected that snow might well be on the way.

'Well, if it does snow,' Miss Fry thought ruefully, 'it can't be helped, but I would rather that it didn't; it could make things most awkward.'

The weather had been exceptionally good that month for December in England, but it was inevitable that it was going to snow eventually. The new year of 1937 seemed destined to be a white one. Miss Fry shivered and looked distastefully up at the sky. She turned to go back inside her room – but found to her horror that there was no handle on the outside of the windows! She was trapped.

The clouds in the sky opened their doors and snow began to fall, brisk and business-like. Miss Fry felt near to tears. She had read in magazine stories of little old ladies going into their gardens in the snow to feed the birds, getting locked out and dying of hypothermia. Previously she had always found these stories rather amusing, but now they no longer seemed funny. Miss Fry began to panic.

'Help! Help!' she started to scream, drumming her fists on the window panes. 'Help! Help!' she continued, her screams turning to croaks.

She turned to look over the balcony again. Perhaps using her stockings and thermal underwear she could make a rope. 'It would be very dangerous,' Miss Fry said, talking aloud as she always did when she was worried. She had no choice – other, that is, than to spend her time weighing up the relative attractions of freezing to death or being dashed to a thousand pieces on the courtyard far below. Miss Fry pulled off her thick hand-knitted stockings and thermal leggings as she wondered if her insurance policy would cover such an escapade. This was the most daring thing that she had done since her jolly-hockey-sticks days at boarding school, when she and several friends had made a rope from their bed sheets in order to climb out of their dormitory window.

'And what a jolly time we had then,' thought Miss Fry. She remembered only the midnight feast in the barn, not the thousand lines and the rap on the knuckles they had all received when caught. She finished securing all the knots and looked proudly at her handiwork. She realized that the rope was not very long and then a flash of inspiration entered her head. She took off her very long tartan scarf and added it to the line.

'Oh dear,' she murmured. 'This is not going to be easy.' She looked over the balcony and started to feel very dizzy. 'I do declare that I suffer from vertigo. How curious, I never did before today. But I mustn't let little things like that put me off. The old girls from school wouldn't have batted an eyelid at this. I'll just pretend to myself that this is our old dorm window.'

Miss Fry tied one end of the rope to a gargoyle which resided at the top of a pillar which was part of the balcony rail. The gargoyle looked as though it were reasonably secure, as secure as something five hundred years old could be. She held on to it for dear life as she gingerly lifted one leg over the balcony edge. She was now astride it as though it were a horse, but her kilt was restricting her as it had become tightly stretched over her two legs; the edge of the material was beginning to cut off the circulation. Miss Fry, with considerable difficulty, managed to put her hands on the ankle that was still on the balcony and yanked her leg over to join the other one. She was now sitting with her legs dangling over the edge. Miss Fry started to feel very sick. It seemed to be a very long, long, long way down.

'Don't jump! Don't jump!' came a loud voice from behind. Before Miss Fry had the chance to look round she felt strong arms on her shoulders and she was pulled unceremoniously back on to the balcony. She fell hard on to the stone floor.

'How dare you!' Miss Fry said angrily as she picked herself up. She was far from grateful.

'Please, you mustn't commit suicide,' said the porter. 'I know the food's bad here but we've never had anyone try and do that before.'

Miss Fry started to laugh helplessly. 'Good heavens!' she exclaimed. 'You didn't think that I was going to . . .? Oh, the very idea!'

'The management of Sir Horace Hedgeworthy would be most grateful if you refrained from doing such a thing here,' the porter continued. He started to sniff again, having recovered from his deed of bravery. 'A suicide could ruin the castle's reputation. A little thing like that could stop us getting into next year's *Good Hotel Guide*.'

'Oh I do apologize,' Miss Fry said sarcastically. 'In future I'll think carefully about where I jump off from. Do you suppose Canterbury Cathedral would mind?'

'I've brought the rest of your luggage up, Miss Fry,' the porter said looking uncomfortable.

'Thank you,' said Miss Fry as she untied the rope from the gargoyle. 'I suppose the silly boy will think that I'm going to hang myself with this,' she thought.

The porter led the way back into the bedroom through the windows. She put the rope down on her bed, meaning to undo it later when she had time. She opened the smallest of the suitcases and took out a rather battered handbag from which she took out an even more battered and cracked leather purse. She extracted a shilling from the purse and gave it to the porter who had his hand outstretched expectantly. 'Do everyone a favour and buy several large cotton handkerchiefs with it,' Miss Fry instructed firmly as the porter sneezed into his other hand.

'Dinner will be served at seven o'clock,' said the porter

as he opened the door to leave. 'The dining room is the last room at the end of this corridor,' he added.

As soon as the young man had gone, Miss Fry ran over to the largest of her suitcases and unlocked it. Inside were seven bottles of French wine, one bottle of vodka, two of brandy, one of sherry and a small silver flask which she usually filled with brandy and kept under the pillow, for those little middle-of-the-night requirements. Miss Fry sank exhausted on to the soft bed. She took the top off the flask and took a long drink of the brandy.

'That's much better!' she declared loudly. 'There's nothing like brandy after a long car journey.' Miss Fry also indulged in large helpings of brandy before a car journey and as a result she usually had to have several cups of strong black coffee at the end of the day.

Miss Fry looked at her wristwatch; it was a quarter to seven. She decided that she had better get dressed for dinner. There was no time to unpack so it was better to leave that for later on in the evening, she thought. She put on the only dress that she knew was suitable for a formal dinner. It was black and almost completely shapeless. She looked in the dressing-table mirror and wondered if it was so suitable after all. She went over to the windows and looked out. It was not yet dark outside, as would usually be expected in late December, but instead appeared very white. The falling flakes of snow were as large as a sixpenny piece. The snow had settled firmly on the ground making a soft white sheet. Miss Fry shivered; a cold breeze was seeping into the room through a small gap where the windows shut. She pulled the red velvet curtains across tightly in order to block it out.

The bedroom was not as regal and grand as perhaps Miss Fry would have liked, for despite the astronomical price it was still one of the cheapest rooms in the castle.

It was quite large but apart from a cupboard, a chest of drawers, a dressing table and the bed, there was no other furniture. The furniture was more or less new, if a little battered, a disappointment to Miss Fry who had hoped to sleep in a bedroom with priceless antiques. True there were several oil paintings and watercolours on the walls but they were of no great quality or beauty. There was no private adjoining bathroom either; there was only one bathroom for each corridor of bedrooms.

Miss Fry had another drink of brandy. If Bournemouth was anything to go by she knew that the standard of the drink at dinner would probably be some port on a melon and a glass of cooking sherry.

Outside the bedroom door, a small man of about five foot four, knelt down at the keyhole. First he put his eye to it but as he could only see the dressing table he replaced it with his rather red and pointed ear. He was a very curious little man, both in appearance and behaviour. He had piercing steely grey eyes and a long black moustache which curled into a circle at each end, making him look a little like a villain from a classic silent film. He was dressed in baggy bright-red trousers, white gym shoes, a black-and-white-striped jersey, a red beret and, most surprising of all, he wore several strings of small onions round his short fat neck. He had a very round stomach, like that of a teddy bear. Despite the altogether unusual nature of these features, there was something about the way they blended together, some indefinable quality, that was really rather appealing. His appearance suggested that he might just happen to be a French onion seller. Either that or a fancy dress party was being held. But what could a French onion seller be doing at an English castle? Perhaps he was an enterprising French onion company representative trying to sell onions to the castle kitchen.

The door opened suddenly and the little man fell into the bedroom and landed on the carpet at Miss Fry's feet. She gave a startled scream; it was not every day that strange men fell at her feet on her opening her bedroom door. She took two steps back in retreat. In several historical romances that she had read, the heroines had been burst in upon while in their bedchambers by handsome enemy soldiers who had carried them off to a faraway castle. The heroine always ended up falling in love with the soldier. Miss Fry looked down anxiously at the little man at her feet. He did not resemble any of the handsome soldiers that she had read about, but one could never tell for certain . . .

'Who are you, sir, and what do you mean by this ungentlemanly intrusion?' demanded Miss Fry. She had a feeling that she had heard that line somewhere before.

'Em . . . em . . .' said the little man, pulling nervously at his moustache.

'Stop fiddling,' commanded Miss Fry, sounding like a schoolmistress.

'Allow me to introduce myself, Madame,' he said with a thick French accent. He got to his feet, and took Miss Fry's hand, bowed and kissed it.

'Oh,' murmured Miss Fry, blushing; her heart missed a beat.

'I am Pierre du Bois,' he announced grandly.

'You're French!' exclaimed Miss Fry delightedly. '*Bonjour monsieur. Je m'appelle, Mademoiselle Fry.*'

'You speak my language with a fine accent,' the man applauded with admiration.

'Oh thank you,' said Miss Fry. She looked coyly at her feet, but made no further attempt to speak French, mainly because she knew little else except, 'Where is the ladies' lavatory?' and that was hardly appropriate.

'I am an onion seller,' said Pierre. 'French onions are

the best in the world; an onion a day keeps the doctor at bay.'

'Oh, a travelling salesman,' muttered Miss Fry, sounding disappointed. The historical heroines never had romances with travelling salesmen. What a pity that this nice Pierre du Bois was not a soldier or even a hangman! Miss Fry recoiled and shook slightly when she suddenly noticed the strings of small French onions round Pierre's plump neck.

'Is anything the matter, Mademoiselle Fry?' asked Pierre, noting the pained grimace on her face. 'A travelling salesman is not such a terrible occupation. There are many perks to it, such as unlimited supplies of pickled onions.'

Miss Fry groaned both inwardly and outwardly at the thought of an unlimited supply of pickled onions, or any onions for that matter.

'Does my choice of career not please you?' asked Pierre looking slightly angry.

'No, no,' Miss Fry assured him, her eyes fixed firmly on the onions, willing them to come no closer.

'Then what is wrong?' Pierre du Bois persisted.

Miss Fry smiled nervously; she had no wish to offend Pierre and his onions. 'It's the onions,' she explained. 'I'm allergic to them. I've no idea why, it's been the same ever since I was a young girl. They make me come out in a horrid rash all over my face and hands. I didn't mean to appear rude, Monsieur du Bois, but I've managed to avoid all contact with onions for over twenty years, and it was quite a shock to have you falling through my doorway with so many round your neck.'

'That's quite all right, Mademoiselle Fry,' Pierre said. He smiled again and looked friendly once more. 'You will of course be at dinner in a few minutes?' He turned and opened the door and left the room.

Miss Fry followed to see him out. 'Yes I will be at dinner,' she confirmed. Pierre started to walk away down the corridor. An urgent thought suddenly occurred to Miss Fry. 'Wait!' she called.

'*Oui?*' questioned Pierre, pausing for a moment.

'Monsieur du Bois, you didn't explain what exactly you were doing kneeling outside my door at the keyhole. I do think that I have the right to expect an explanation.'

'Mademoiselle, the answer to that is simple,' said Pierre airily as he walked away. 'I was merely checking your bedroom door for woodworm.' He opened the dining-room door and went in.

Miss Fry watched him go, shaking her head in amazement. She had never met anyone like Pierre du Bois before. She went back into her bedroom to collect her evening bag.

'Oh dear,' she said aloud, realization of what she had done dawning on her. She looked nervously up at the heavens, half expecting to be struck down. 'I've had a strange man in my bedroom! A foreign man at that! Daddy must be turning in his grave – well he would be if he hadn't been cremated!'

Miss Fry, remembering the onions, ran over to the dressing table to take a look at herself in the mirror. She could see a faint rash appearing over the bridge of her nose and cheeks. She sighed dispiritedly, sank on to her bed and picked up the silver flask. She drank heavily. 'What a day it's been so far, what a day,' she muttered as she drank.

Chapter Three

iss Fry, having recovered, left her bedroom. The rash was slightly worse but with any luck no one would notice. She wondered, not for the first time, why the heroines in her beloved historical romances never had allergies and always had perfect milk-white skin. She wished that there was a lock on her bedroom door; as there was not, she had had to put all her drink in the suitcase again. When in Bournemouth one year, she had had a most horrendous embarrassment the memory of which still made her shudder. At that particular boarding house a maid did all the guests' unpacking. The maid had unpacked Miss Fry's alcohol suitcase which she had not thought to lock. So within hours, the entire staff and guests had been told about the suitcase and its contents. The whispering and giggling had been intolerable and Miss Fry had left the boarding house the following morning, never to return. It was hardly surprising that Miss Fry felt a little nervous as she entered the dining room. She had after all never moved in such social circles and she realized that only the very wealthy could afford the prices at Waddington Castle.

Although taught the social graces – such as deportment, practised with the aid of six books on her head – at boarding school, she was worried that she might be out of date or that she might have forgotten things; and there had been so many things that it had been considered imperative to know. Like how the upper class folded their napkins, which knife and fork to use and how a real lady never drank more than one glass of wine per day. Yes, Miss Fry had certainly forgotten some of the more important things taught at school.

The dining room was long and narrow. It was very dark, lit by a small chandelier in the centre of the ceiling, and by a candlestick in the centre of the table. Miss Fry sat down. The table was long; it could easily have seated twenty-five, but including Miss Fry now sat only seven. There were fine oil paintings on the walls. Miss Fry recognized one to be a Van Gogh, but guessed that this must only be a very clever copy since the original hung in the Louvre – at least it had until it had been stolen not so long ago.

Around the sides of the room were sideboards on which were exhibited small statues that looked Greek in origin. Miss Fry, who was a very clean and tidy person, noted with slight irritation that the ceiling and sideboards had cobwebs and dust on them. On the ceiling directly above Miss Fry was a large, black, hairy-legged spider. She eyed it with fear, and as most ladies in her position would, she shook. Silently she prayed that the spider would not suddenly decide to descend on to her head during dinner. It was as she stared at the spider, as though to ward it off, that she noticed that she herself was being stared at, by the other guests sitting at the long table.

'How do you do?' she said, smiling politely. When at boarding school, she and the other girls, during their 'Charm and Politeness' classes, had always been told to start a conversation with strangers in this way. 'I am Miss Fry.'

'How do you do?' the other six people chorused politely. Evidently they had also attended 'Charm and Politeness' lessons.

'I think that introductions are in order,' said one of the men. 'I am General Habinger.' He looked and sounded every inch an English army general. His voice was gruff, but not too fierce, and he had a fine bristling moustache. He wore a green uniform and medals from the First World War with obvious pride. He was aged somewhere between fifty-five and sixty-five.

'I am Miss Fry,' said Miss Fry, forgetting that she had already told them that.

'I'm glad to see that you're English,' General Habinger confided. 'There are spies everywhere . . . foreigners!' Miss Fry stared. Perhaps this was not a genuine army officer after all, and instead he was a dangerous lunatic who had escaped from an asylum.

'Spies? . . . foreigners?' she asked cautiously.

'Germans, of course!' the General exclaimed. He banged the prongs of his fork on to the table, making a deep dent.

'Oh, of course,' Miss Fry humoured. 'Germans.'

'I am sure that there will not be another war with Germany,' Pierre du Bois said quietly. His voice, compared with General Habinger's gruff tones, had a quiet dignity to it.

'Great Scott!' General Habinger cried, jumping to his feet, mistaking Pierre's accent for German rather than French. 'He's German! There's no mistaking one, I can tell by his eyes and his voice. I shot dead hundreds of them in the war and they all had a certain look in their eyes, and he's got it. I tell you I shot hundreds of 'em.'

'A most admirable accomplishment, I'm sure,' a young

woman with blonde hair and black roots said with sarcasm.

'Thank you my dear,' General Habinger said, oblivious of the woman's sarcasm. Like many people he took all compliments at face value, and it never occurred to him that some were not intended. 'The question is,' the General continued, eyeing Pierre with suspicion, 'what do we do with this dastardly spy?'

'I don't wish to spoil your fun, but I really do think that I must tell you that I am not a spy, nor am I German. I am Pierre du Bois. I am of French nationality and for a living I am a salesman,' said Pierre. He did not appear to be at all ruffled by the accusations thrown at him, and instead seemed to be amused. He explained his social status as though he were a nursery-school teacher talking to his class.

'I really do think that General Habinger owes poor Pierre an apology,' the blonde woman said.

'French, eh?' the General said, looking shrewdly at Pierre through a monocle which he took from his jacket pocket. He did not seem to have heard the woman's recommendation, but then he was the sort of man who heard what he chose to. 'Could have sworn that you were German; those eyes and the accent.'

'I've been to France myself,' Miss Fry said. 'I've never noticed any similarities between French and German accents. Though of course I'm no expert; the only Germans I've ever seen were in one of those American war films, and that was nearly two years ago now.'

'French,' General Habinger repeated thoughtfully, more to himself than anyone else. 'Never trusted the French, always been in league with the Germans if you ask me.' No one contradicted him. He was not the sort of man who would listen and if he did he would be angry, so no one made the effort.

'I sell onions,' Pierre said fingering the strings of them round his neck. 'They are not expensive so if any of you wish to make an order . . .?'

There was an enthusiastic silence. Everyone looked up at the ceiling or at the paintings on the wall in order to avoid Pierre's gaze. Although each of the guests was comfortably well off, they were prudent, if not plain mean, where French onions were concerned.

'We didn't finish our introductions,' the blonde said, partly to remind them all and partly to break the uneasy silence. 'I'm Joan Summers and this . . .' she said prodding the young man next to her, 'is my husband Edmund.'

'Hello folks,' said Edmund looking bored. He was a young, lean man who was good looking in a faintly untrustworthy sort of way.

Sitting next to the General was a woman in her late fifties. 'I'm Mrs Williams.' She had light-blue hair, as she seemed to have followed the curious fashion that old ladies have of using light-blue or pink rinses. She was plump and matronly and it was not too difficult to tell that she already knew General Habinger, since she had cast several adoring glances in his direction.

'And I'm just a simple vicar,' said the last of the people at the table, 'I'm Reverend Peters.' He was in his late fifties, with short white hair which was going thin on the top of his head. He wore black trousers, black shirt, a black jacket, a white dog collar and a large wooden cross on a silver chain round his neck.

'How do you do, Reverend?' said Miss Fry. She was glad that at least one of the guests had a respectable occupation. She had not dared to look directly at Pierre du Bois, for fear that he might refer to the incident earlier. What would the others say if they knew that she had had a strange foreign man in her bedroom without a formal introduction? What a terrible thing to have happened! The Women's Institute would have been shocked at Miss Fry's apparent lack of morality.

'So you sell onions, do you,' said General Habinger to Pierre. 'I wondered why you had strings of them around your neck. I thought that they must be for warding off vampires.'

'That's garlic,' Reverend Peters corrected. 'In my old parish we all used to hang wreaths of garlic on our front doors at night.'

'Oh?' said Joan with interest. 'Was that because you and your parishioners believed in vampires?'

'It was far more than mere belief,' Reverend Peters said mysteriously.

'Oh do tell us about it,' said Mrs Williams enthusiastically.

'Yes, do,' agreed General Habinger as he lit his pipe. 'I always enjoy a good yarn. It'll be something to pass the time while *we wait for those damn servants to serve dinner*!' The last words he shouted loudly, as if in the hope that the servants would hear. At that very moment, just as the General was about to bang his fork down on to the table, the dining-room door opened. The receptionist came into the room, but she was now dressed in the uniform of a maid. She was followed by a tall, well-built man who was obviously the butler. Both carried large trays with the first course. 'About time,' muttered the General. He watched intently, like a hawk, as the first course was served.

'Reverend Peters, you were telling us about your parishioners and their beliefs in the wonders of garlic,' Edmund reminded. 'Pray, do continue!'

Reverend Peters, not noticing Edmund's attempt at a pun, looked nervously at the butler and the maid. 'I say, do you think I ought, right now . . . in front of . . .'

'Do carry on,' prompted Joan. She was certain that the

37

vicar had nothing so confidential to say that it could not be said in front of the staff.

He paused a moment, but his concern for privacy was alleviated when the butler and maid left the room, presumably to make ready the second course.

'When I left my parish,' Reverend Peters started darkly, 'there were no parishioners left. One by one they were bitten, buried and rose again.'

'The resurrection?' suggested Mrs Williams.

'No . . . indeed, no,' the vicar replied, sweat breaking out on his brow. 'They rose . . . as . . . vampires!'

There was an embarrassed silence. Everybody stared at everybody else; all exchanged raised eyebrows and quizzical looks. Everyone wondered if they were eating dinner with a psychopathic maniac. All played nervously with their food, pretending that they were uninterested and only half listening. Edmund tapped a finger on the side of his head, pointing meaningfully at Reverend Peters.

'I can see that you don't believe me,' Reverend Peters said with a sad, patient, understanding smile. 'I can hardly blame you, I didn't believe until it was far, far too late. A vampire had been buried in our churchyard several hundred years ago. Last year there was a freak storm and a flash of fork lightning struck the tomb, causing the vampire to wake up.

'You probably know that traditionally a vampire is laid to rest by driving a stake into the heart, cutting the body into quarters and pouring garlic and holy water down the throat: all the same, it only took about six days for some of the villagers to start saying that the vampire had risen. A girl had teeth marks on her neck and they claimed that she was receiving nightly visits from a blood-sucking vampire. They told me, but I was convinced that they were love bites from a boyfriend. However when the girl died and two more girls were found to have the same marks, I had to decide whether they were victims of an over-enthusiastic boyfriend or a vampire. I chose the latter; no boy has teeth like that. The villagers came to me again, this time demanding that we exhume the body and give it the vampire treatment; assuming that there was a body, by rights there should only have been bones.'

'Good heavens!' exclaimed Miss Fry.

'Indeed,' Reverend Peters continued, now in full swing. 'Well, I couldn't authorize such an action so I went to the Archbishop of Canterbury but he told me that he couldn't authorize it either. He took me to the highest authority in the land, the head of the Church of England.'

'Good God!' exclaimed General Habinger.

'No, the King,' corrected Reverend Peters. He wiped his perspiring brow with his red-and-white-spotted handkerchief. 'The King gave us tea and crumpets in his sitting room . . .'

'Fancy that!' said Joan. 'Did you have Mrs Simpson there too?'

'No, just tea and crumpets,' replied Reverend Peters, wishing that everyone would be quiet and allow him to tell his story. He did not follow royal gossip and thought that Mrs Simpson must be a type of cake. 'The King fell off his chair, dropping tea all over himself, when we explained the situation to him.'

'Because he was so moved by your touching story?' asked Mrs Williams, lighting a cigarette.

'No, he couldn't stop laughing,' said Reverend Peters looking slightly embarrassed. 'He didn't give his permission I'm afraid.'

'Well that's believable,' said Edmund with a laugh.

'What happened next?' asked Joan.

'You should have got the army in and bombed the little blighter!' said General Habinger constructively.

'Blighters,' Reverend Peters corrected. 'Each of the vampire's victims in turn became a vampire.'

'It's a wonder that there was enough blood to go round,' Edmund said flippantly. 'Still I expect God provided!'

'Please, I beg of you, do not jest,' Reverend Peters reproved gravely. 'Soon I was the only person in the village who was alive. I had to desert my parish because there were no parishioners, and, alas, because I am in no hurry to go to heaven.'

'How dreadful!' Miss Fry said with sympathy. 'And are you now out of a job?'

'I'm going to be the Archbishop's new secretary, but first of all I'm spending the New Year here in an attempt to recover. Not that I can ever hope to.'

'No of course not,' agreed Miss Fry. 'I can't remember reading about any of this in *The Times*.'

'I do not believe that it would have appealed to any of the newspapers,' said Reverend Peters.

'Oh, I don't know about that,' said Edmund. 'I'm a reporter and I'm certain that this sort of story would be right up Fleet Street's street. In fact if you care to give me an interview, Rev, I could give you a jolly decent write-up.'

'If you don't mind, Edmund old chap, I would rather not,' said Reverend Peters cautiously, as he did not wish to offend. 'I'm rather anxious to avoid publicity, I mean it's not as though I were trying to raise money to mend a church steeple, is it?'

'Hum . . .' Edmund said, reluctant to let go. 'Perhaps tomorrow or the next day we can come to some arrangement. We could do an anonymous interview, saying that you were living in fear of being followed by vengeful vampires.'

'But that's just it,' said Reverend Peters, looking as though he might burst into tears at any moment. 'I am living in dire fear of being followed by those devil-possessed vampires.' There was an uneasy silence among the guests again, as they tried to determine whether the vicar was crazy or not.

'Well I hope that you've got plenty of garlic with you then,' said Edmund, in a poor attempt at a joke. No one laughed.

'I wonder if it's still snowing outside,' said Miss Fry. The butler and maid came back at this moment to serve the main course just as she was looking out of the window. 'It is,' she informed them. 'It is extremely thick. I don't believe that we could get out even if we wanted to.'

'It's quite cold, isn't it?' Joan observed.

'Why exactly did you come to Waddington Castle, Miss Fry?' Edmund asked curiously. 'I wouldn't have thought that seeing the New Year in with a group of strangers would be your idea of fun.'

'Well, you're right, in that I've never done anything like this before,' smiled Miss Fry as she returned to the table. The butler and maid, having served the main course, left the room.

Miss Fry continued, 'My father died last month and . . .'

'Oh what a coincidence,' interrupted Mrs Williams. 'My father's dead too!'

'Really?' Miss Fry said, showing a distinct lack of interest. 'We lived together and were very close right up until the end. When he died I decided to take a break away from everything to plan out my future. But I would have thought that this was more my type of place than somewhere for a young married couple like yourself and Joan. After all, the rest of us are hardly your age group.'

Joan smiled weakly and looked at Edmund. 'Oh, I don't know, we thought that we would like a short break in a hotel with a difference. Well, you can't get a more unusual hotel than this one. I've never heard of a castle used like this.'

'How did your father die, Miss Fry?' Mrs Williams asked.

'He fell off a cliff,' Miss Fry replied shortly.

'Oh, how . . . how tragic,' Mrs Williams said, virtually lost for words. What did one say to a woman whose father had fallen off a cliff the previous month?

'He wasn't pushed, was he?' Edmund asked hopefully. He was scribbling furiously in a large notebook.

'No, he was not!' Miss Fry said forcefully. 'He was walking our dog on the cliff top, but the wind was gale force and he was swept over the edge and smashed to pieces. The rocks below still bear the marks of his blood.'

Mrs Williams gasped and her face turned a little green. She clapped a hand over her mouth, fearful that she might be sick.

'What about the dog?' Joan asked with concern. 'Was he all right?'

'No, he was smashed too,' replied Miss Fry. By now she sounded as though she were just discussing the weather.

'Would you care for a sherry, gentlemen?' General Habinger enquired, pouring himself a generous measure.

'Thank you,' Reverend Peters said, pushing his glass forward. Edmund passed his glass along and so did Joan. The General stared with disapproval through his monocle at Joan and after a moment's pause, poured a small measure for her; the idea of a woman drinking! Mrs Williams looked as though she would have liked a glass of sherry but glancing at General Habinger seemed to change her mind.

'Miss Fry?' asked Edmund politely.

'Goodness no, thank you.' Miss Fry looked shocked at such an improper suggestion. She shot a quick look at

Joan. 'Somehow it has never seemed quite ladylike to drink alcohol, even in private,' she remarked.

'Then I guess I'm no lady!' laughed Joan, draining her glass. 'But that's my limit. I agree that it certainly isn't proper for a lady to drink to excess.'

'What are you doing, Edmund?' Reverend Peters asked.

'Oh, nothing in particular,' Edmund replied, quickly shutting his notebook and putting his fountain pen away in his dinner-jacket pocket.

'Come, come,' said Reverend Peters smiling. If he had been sitting next to Edmund he would have patted him on the head. 'There's no need to be bashful, my boy, I know exactly what you were doing.'

'You . . . you do?' came the cautious, slightly worried reply. 'What?'

'Poetry!' Reverend Peters continued with enthusiasm. 'As soon as I saw you, I thought to myself, that boy looks like a poet.'

'Whatever made you think that he looked like a poet?' asked Mrs Williams in amusement.

'I can tell. It's a gift, I suppose, second sight as it were. Look at his jaw bone: all poets have a weak jaw bone, it represents their sensitivity and vulnerability. He has a startling resemblance to the poet William Blake.'

'Steady on, Reverend,' Edmund interrupted. 'Wasn't he the one who wrote lots of religious stuff and was a bit mad? I saw some of his etchings once and they looked like the work of a nutcase rather than that of a poet.'

'Well all poets have a touch of madness in them, don't they? You may be surprised to know that I write a little poetry myself. Perhaps you would care to read through some of it with me tomorrow?' continued the vicar. 'I'm afraid that it isn't very good though.'

'You're just being modest, I'm sure,' Mrs Williams said. 'Perhaps you should write some poetry about your horrendous experiences with the vampires,' suggested Edmund, trying to suppress a giggle.

'I write mainly about the feelings of furniture,' Reverend Peters replied. He had no idea that the vampire suggestion was made merely in jest. 'We misuse and abuse our chairs and tables and the like, without any regard for their thoughts and feelings.'

Everyone looked discreetly away. All of them were certain that the Reverend Peters was not a well man. Most of them put it down to his nerve-shattering ordeal in his last parish, but some disbelieved everything he had told them and thought him a little mad.

'It was poetry that you were writing was it, Edmund?' Miss Fry asked. She had a suspicion that he was concealing something.

'What? . . . oh, yes of course it was,' he replied.

'Damn funny thing for a man to do,' commented General Habinger. 'Effeminate if you ask me.'

'You've been very quiet, Monsieur du Bois,' said Miss Fry. 'Do you write at all?'

'Flower arranging and taxidermy are my interests,' replied Pierre, ending his long silence.

'Taxidermy!' exclaimed the delighted Miss Fry. 'How wonderful. It's my passion too! I was taking a course in it at the local college shortly before my father died. I only just had time to complete it . . .'

'No doubt everyone will think me very ignorant,' interrupted Reverend Peters. 'But what exactly is taxidermy?'

'The art of stuffing,' Joan said. She was painstakingly applying gaudy pink nail varnish.

'Stuffing?' the vicar asked, confused. Coming from a well-educated religious background he was surprisingly unworldly in some matters. 'Stuffing as in roast chicken?'

Joan giggled. 'No! Stuffing as in preserving. You know, stuffing dead animals for display?'

After tea and digestive biscuits, the group transferred to the comfortable sitting room for further tea and biscuits; except that is for General Habinger, who decided to get straight to bed, and Mrs Williams who professed herself tired too a few moments later. The sitting room was medium sized, with cream satin curtains, Victorian furniture, Persian carpets and several paintings by Turner and Gainsborough. Miss Fry had fetched from her bedroom *The Hangman and the Nursemaid* and, having settled in a soft armchair in front of the blazing log fire, proceeded to read it. During the first six pages the heroine's father was murdered, her mother ran away with a woodcutter and she was cast on to the streets of the cruel world by the mercenary landlord of her cottage because she had no money to pay the rent and would not pay it in personal services. Such heartbreak and deep tragedy soon had Miss Fry reaching for her lace handkerchief. After ten pages of the heroine's misery, the delicate lace handkerchief was wringing wet with tears of pure enjoyment.

'What are you reading, Miss Fry?' asked Edmund. He was sitting in the opposite armchair writing furiously in his notebook.

'*The Hangman and the Nursemaid*,' a dewy-eyed Miss Fry answered, looking up. 'It's wonderful.'

'Historical novels, eh?' Edmund said, raising an eyebrow. 'I came to the conclusion some years ago that people who read them usually tend to live in the past.'

'There's nothing wrong with liking the old days – is there?' Miss Fry asked cautiously. She felt nervous and had the feeling that this could turn out to be an interrogation like that of the Women's Institute. Miss Fry, although terrified, like everyone else, of the Institute, was determined not to stand any nonsense from this impertinent young man.

'I've always found that people who live in the past

cannot face up to the realities of change in the modern world. They often crack under the pressure or expect everyone to live as though we were Tudors,' said Edmund. He was now sitting forward at the edge of his chair, and his face was close to Miss Fry's who was also now sitting forward in her armchair.

'I don't know what you are trying to get at, young man,' Miss Fry said fiercely, her eyes flashing with anger. 'But whatever it is . . . you're not getting there!'

'Edmund!' cried Joan, jumping up from the sofa. She stepped in between Miss Fry and her husband so that he was forced to look at her instead. 'I'm shocked at your bad manners. How could you be so horrid to someone you only met for the first time this evening? Apologize to Miss Fry at once.'

'Sorry,' Edmund said shortly and flatly. 'If you want to live in the past, Miss Fry, you go right ahead.'

Miss Fry went red with anger, shut her book with a bang and stood up. 'It's half past ten and I'm going to bed.' She left the room, slamming the door behind her.

'Did I upset her?' asked Edmund, with wonder.

Miss Fry was not really very sleepy, she had just been unable to take any more of Edmund's insults. 'Oh I could hit him for saying such nasty things!' she thought to herself violently, as she marched down the corridor. 'Young men simply were not like that when I was young; one could always count on a chap for compliments, chocolates, flowers and jewels. Of course Mother always said that I wasn't to accept the jewels as that would seem like I was being bought, but of course I always did. As for that Edmund, he may be married but he could have at least paid me a compliment.'

Miss Fry opened the first door that she came to without thinking as she was so annoyed. She went inside shutting it behind her. It was dark and she fumbled around on the wall for the light switch but was unable to find it. She then began to panic! What if there was a strange man in the room? She would not mind that too much if he looked like a romantic Arab sheik like her film idol Rudolph Valentino! Supposing the castle was haunted! Miss Fry was now frightened and ran out of the room shaking with fear. Once out of the room she began to giggle nervously, like a schoolgirl who had been trying to frighten herself. Miss Fry, without the strict discipline of her father, had begun to rejuvenate.

Upon reaching her bedroom, Miss Fry noticed that the door of the room next to hers was partly open. Being very nosy she stood still and stared in. General Habinger was sitting on a chair polishing a revolver and appeared to be talking to it with fondness. Miss Fry found nothing odd about this, she often spoke to her favourite possessions. Miss Fry went along to her own bedroom, a thoughtful look on her face. 'I wish I had a gun, such useful things; one just never knows when one might come in handy,' she mused to herself.

After her nightcap, she got into bed for what she hoped would be a peaceful night. Just before falling asleep she heard a man and woman shouting from down the hallway. She thought it sounded like Joan and Edmund and strained her ears in order to try and make out the words.

'I want a divorce!' the woman demanded.

Miss Fry sat up in bed. This sounded distinctly interesting.

'A divorce?' the man questioned, sounding mildly surprised.

'Yes, a divorce,' the woman continued. 'I've just realized that I was crazy to marry you. I should have listened to Mother and married the Duke of Hastings when I had the chance. You told me that you were a millionaire!'

47

'I am,' the man protested. 'Do keep your voice down Joan, people might hear.'

'I don't care if people do hear; it's about time people heard the truth about you. Millionaire indeed! I should never have believed you. I've never heard of a journalist millionaire but then there probably isn't such a thing except in your imagination. Have you seen the state of your socks? What self-respecting millionaire has holes in his socks?'

'I'm eccentric,' Edmund declared.

'Oh, and I suppose eccentrics don't believe in spending money on their wives?' Joan asked angrily.

'We can't get divorced,' Edmund said, sounding appalled at the idea. 'It isn't the done thing. People won't invite us to parties, we'll become social outcasts and Daddy will cut me off without a penny. I'm sorry, but I won't do it.'

'Why not?' asked Joan, sounding slightly hysterical.

'I can't afford it,' he replied. 'Moneywise or socially.'

There was a loud crash and the sound of breaking glass. 'You idiot,' cried Edmund. 'You've broken the window.'

'It was your fault for jumping out of the way,' shouted Joan, sounding murderous.

'Let's get out of here before the maid or someone comes along. I don't want any more money added to our bill,' said Edmund.

There came the sound of footsteps as Edmund dragged Joan away from the scene of the crime. Miss Fry shook her head with wonder. 'Dear, dear me,' she murmured. People had not behaved in that way when she was young. As she thought about the young people of today, she dropped off to sleep.

Chapter Four

The grandfather clock in the hallway struck midnight. Then there was silence except for the steady ticking of the clock. Suddenly there came a woman's blood-curdling scream. At once everyone who was asleep woke up, put on their dressing gowns and ran out of their rooms. Someone switched the hall light on.

'What's happened?' several of the guests asked.

On the floor, lying face down, was a body in full evening wear. An axe was firmly implanted in the man's back, and from the wound blood was steadily dripping down on to the white goatskin rug, making a most becoming pattern. Joan was kneeling down over the body sobbing distraughtly. She had obviously not been to bed since she was also still wearing her clothes from dinner.

'Who is it?' asked General Habinger, hurriedly putting his monocle to his eye. He was wearing emerald-coloured silk pyjamas embroidered with little cannons and a dressing gown to match. The others could not help but notice that he and Mrs Williams had come out of the same bedroom. Shocking behaviour!

'It's Edmund!' Joan sobbed.

'Is he dead?' asked Miss Fry, who it seemed had no experience in these matters.

'With an axe in the middle of his back I would say that it is a fair cert,' Pierre commented.

Joan stood up and promptly fainted into a rather startled Reverend Peters's arms.

'I suggest that we go into the drawing room and talk this over,' suggested Reverend Peters, his arms severely strained by Joan's weight. 'If we're lucky perhaps the maid can supply some hot chocolate and digestive biscuits.' He seemed to be unaffected by the bloody body at his feet, but perhaps his former training as a Benedictine monk served him in good stead.

'To hell with hot chocolate!' snorted the General. 'A good whisky for me.'

'What . . . what about Edmund?' asked Miss Fry.

'Leave him,' instructed General Habinger. 'I'm sure he won't walk away.'

With Mrs Williams's help, Reverend Peters dragged Joan into the drawing room and laid her down on the sofa. Pierre du Bois lit the oil lamps and unlocked the drinks cabinet. Miss Fry took a drink along with the others, for the moment not caring whether it was ladylike or not to drink in public. Joan made weak motions with her arms as she started to come round. Mrs Williams, being an enterprising woman but having no smelling salts with her, took a carnation from a nearby vase and placed it under Joan's nose.

When Joan opened her eyes, everyone was sitting in a semicircle around her, watching with great interest and anticipation. By the time she opened her mouth to speak everyone had noticed that her eyes were the colour of sapphires, her eyebrows severely plucked into a thin arch and her eyelashes caked with mascara – which had now travelled down her cheeks.

'What happened?' asked Reverend Peters.

'Ed . . . Edmund . . . he's dead!' she sobbed hysterically.

'Allow me to console you with the thought that God has taken him to a far better place,' Reverend Peters said, putting his arm round Joan's shoulder in a way that Miss Fry considered a little too familiar.

'We must conduct this as though it were a police enquiry,' General Habinger said as he drained his glass, refilled it and stood up. 'As a high-ranking military officer it seems to be the natural procedure for me to take charge.'

'I do not see why, monsieur,' commented Pierre who quite fancied himself in that position.

'I'm certainly more qualified to do so than an onion seller,' snapped General Habinger. 'And a foreign onion seller at that.'

'If you don't mind my saying so,' Reverend Peters said, 'don't you think that we should be telephoning the police so that they can take charge? I don't suppose that they have ever had a murder in Waddington so I daresay they will be delighted to come over at once and investigate.'

General Habinger looked mutinous but he knew that it was his duty as an officer and a gentleman to make the call. 'Very well,' he muttered, draining his glass for the second time.

The telephone was on the coffee table. Mrs Williams picked up the receiver and handed it to the General. The others were all too preoccupied with their own thoughts to notice the adoring gaze Mrs Williams gave him, all, that is, apart from Pierre who watched closely.

'Hello, operator?' General Habinger barked into the telephone. 'Hello? . . . Operator? . . . How strange.' He put the receiver down and turned to the others who were watching him anxiously. Joan continued to cry uncontrollably. 'It appears to be . . . dead.'

Mrs Williams screamed and dropped her glass to the ground where it smashed into a thousand tiny fragments. 'The wires have been cut!' she cried, her eyes wild like a horse's with fear. 'I saw it happen in a film. The wires were cut and the people in the house were murdered in their beds, one by one! We're doomed, doomed!' Having completed her outburst she collapsed in tears on to one of the armchairs.

There was an embarrassed silence – apart from Joan's and Mrs Williams's sobbing – as everyone pretended that nothing had happened. General Habinger gingerly placed one hand on Mrs Williams's shoulder but removed it when she jumped and gave him an accusing glare.

'It's all right!' Miss Fry exclaimed, relieved at being able to break the deathly quiet. 'It must be the weather; the snow's brought the telephone wires down.'

Everyone who was not crying heaved a sigh of relief. Mrs Williams blew her nose, dabbed her eyes and made some effort to achieve a degree of composure.

'It appears, General Habinger,' Reverend Peters remarked, 'that you will have to head tonight's enquiry.'

'Why do we have to have an enquiry?' Miss Fry asked. 'Can't we just go to bed?'

'Indeed not,' Reverend Peters said gravely. 'A man has been murdered and we must attempt to ascertain who the culprit is in order to place him under lock and key tonight, so that we can sleep safely in our beds.'

'How can you be so sure that it was murder?' asked a wide-eyed Miss Fry.

'With a hulking great axe in the middle of his back it could hardly be suicide,' Joan snapped bitterly.

'Our first suspect is, I fear, Mrs Joan Summers,' said General Habinger with sincere regret. 'Mainly because you are the only one here who knew him before tonight and could possibly have had a motive. If you will pardon this question, but . . . were you happily married?'

'Not . . . not exactly,' admitted Joan slowly. She seemed unwilling to discuss it any further. She had stopped crying now and instead had lit a cigarette.

'Hang on a tick!' exclaimed Miss Fry. She now recalled having been disturbed before falling asleep. 'Before I drifted into slumberland I heard a man and woman fighting like a cat and dog outside my bedroom door. Was it you and Edmund?'

Joan appeared at first to be about to deny it but changed her mind. 'Yes . . . yes it was, but I really don't see how this is going to help us to determine which of you murdered my husband.'

'Can you remember what the conversation was about, Miss Fry?' asked Pierre. He was wearing blue-and-white-striped pyjamas but no onions adorned his neck this time.

'Yes,' said Miss Fry, looking thoughtful as she sat down beside Joan. 'I was sitting up in bed; I was just about to put my hair rollers in, when I heard the most ghastly racket coming from the corridor outside. Naturally I didn't intend to eavesdrop, as that would have been very rude, but they were shouting so loudly that I couldn't help but overhear. I'm positive that they were Joan and Edmund.'

'Yes, but what did they talk about?' asked General Habinger impatiently, wishing that Miss Fry would hurry up and get on with it. 'Or rather what were they arguing about?'

'The woman wanted a divorce,' Miss Fry continued slowly. She was rather enjoying the fact that all in the room were giving her their full attention. 'She was also angry because her husband had socks full of holes and had claimed to be a millionaire before their marriage, so marrying her under false pretences.'

'Well, Joan?' Pierre said sternly.

'Excuse me,' General Habinger said huffily. 'I ask the questions. Mrs Summers, was the conversation Miss Fry heard between you and Edmund?'

'Yes,' admitted Joan. She looked and sounded very irritated. 'But if you're trying to insinuate that I murdered Edmund you're wrong. What would be my motive?'

'He wouldn't give you a divorce,' Miss Fry said, appearing suddenly to recall the rest of the conversation. 'Edmund said that he couldn't afford it, socially or financially. And he said that he would be disinherited by his father.'

'Mrs Summers,' General Habinger said gravely. 'The evidence is all against you. What better place to kill an unwanted partner than at an hotel where no one knows you? For all we know you may have registered here under a false name. You could have left Waddington tomorrow morning, leaving the body here.'

Joan started to choke, partly because she had smoked several cigarettes far too quickly, partly because she was shocked by the accusations.

'I've never heard of anything so preposterous!' Joan at last spluttered. 'Do you really think that if I had murdered Edmund I would have screamed, so waking every single person in this wing?'

The General looked somewhat stumped. He was not used to having people answer back, and certainly not a woman! He twirled the ends of his moustache for want of something to say.

'Well that's jolly easy to answer,' said Miss Fry, having waited a moment to see if General Habinger would speak. During the charm classes at school she and her schoolgirl chums had always been taught that when theories were being presented for murder, they should always allow gentlemen to present theirs first. If a girl spoke too soon

54

she might not be invited to other parties where murders were committed and, even worse, she might then not get any proposals of marriage.

'Well?' asked the General.

'We are, as you all know, completely cut off due to the snow. Joan, knowing this, would not be able to stick to her original plan of murdering Edmund and leaving the body here because we are snowed in. Being devilish clever, Joan killed him with the axe and then screamed so that we would believe her to be innocent and look for another suspect.'

'These accusations are nothing short of ludicrous,' Joan said standing up. 'And I refuse to sit here and listen to them.' She lit another cigarette, this time putting it into an ebony holder and started to walk out of the room.

'I'm sorry,' General Habinger said. He put a firm hand on Joan's arm. 'But since you are the only one of us here who has a motive, I feel that it is my duty to put you under citizen's arrest.'

'What!' Joan exclaimed, flabbergasted.

'I do think you are being a little bit hasty, General,' Pierre du Bois said quietly, but no one seemed or wanted to take any notice.

'Since there are no keys for the bedrooms we will lock you in here,' General Habinger continued.

'All of you have motives too,' started Joan. 'I'll tell you why Edmund and I were here . . .'

'We will talk further in the morning, when we have contacted the police,' General Habinger interrupted firmly. He signalled for the other guests to get up and leave the room and despite Joan's protest he also left the room, locking the door behind him. Joan flung herself down on to the sofa and burst into tears. She was now alone.

Chapter Five

 iss Fry yawned, stretched and opened her eyes, in that order. She turned her head to look at the travelling clock, which she took everywhere with her and which was standing on the bedside table. It had just turned five past seven. She sat up, yawned again, and delved under her pillow to retrieve the drinking flask; there was, after all, nothing like a stiff drink to start the day! Having satisfied her thirst she jumped out of bed, in so energetic a way that it quite surprised her; such a vigorous jump she had thought impossible at her age.

With a start, she suddenly remembered the events of the previous night. She shook her head with wonder. Nothing like this had ever happened at Penton; what would the Women's Institute say? Miss Fry had had little excitement in her life and she was finding all this most exhilarating. Perhaps, she reasoned, this had something to do with her secret gypsy ancestry – though quite what it had to do with it she did not know. She pulled the curtains and stared out of the window. 'It looks like a Christmas card!' she breathed with delight. And so it did. The snow, for the moment, had stopped, but the land for miles around was covered with a thick blanket of white. Miss Fry was in little doubt that the castle was completely cut off from the village of Waddington. 'I wonder what is to be done with that young girl Joan?' she said aloud . . .

As there was only one bathroom between all of the guests Miss Fry knew that there would inevitably be a rush at eight o'clock. Miss Fry put on her dressing gown and picked up the telephone to call down to the desk.

'Hello? . . . yes, this is Miss Fry. Could you please run my bath for me . . . I will have it directly and I want plenty of carbolic soap and lots of bubbly . . . no not champagne, bubble bath! Knock on my door when it's ready. Thank you very much.'

Miss Fry took a look at herself in the dressing-table mirror and groaned. It was not a very pretty sight. Ever since she had been nine years old she had dreamed of growing up to be a beautiful young woman who would marry a handsome young gypsy and they would live happily ever after in a gypsy caravan. The vision she saw in the mirror was neither young nor beautiful. She could not help realizing that perhaps she was a little too old to be carried off by a handsome young gypsy and being used to modern conveniences she was not at all sure that she would enjoy living in a caravan. She picked up her historical romance novel and retreated within the pages of fantasy where everyone was young, beautiful and often a gypsy.

Miss Fry dropped her book with a crash when there came a sudden ear-piercing scream from the direction of the bathroom. She jumped up, tripping over her dressing-gown cord as she went, and ran out of the room. The other guests had also been awakened and were now crowding into the tiny bathroom.

'What's happened, what's happened?' asked Miss Fry, running to join them.

'I don't advise you to go in, Miss Fry,' Reverend Peters cautioned. 'This is no sight for a lady.'

'Nonsense!' cried Miss Fry, barging past him. She stared with fascination down into the bathtub. A woman, still in her nightclothes, was lying face down in the bath, which was full of water. It was fairly easy for them to deduce that the woman, who was clearly dead, was Mrs Williams, due to the blue hair rinse which had now discoloured the water.

'Is she dead?' General Habinger asked in a somewhat strangulated voice.

'Looks that way,' said Miss Fry cheerfully. 'What a pity that none of us knew her properly. What is her name again, or rather what was her name?'

'Mrs Williams,' said Pierre rather curtly. Then, fixing General Habinger with his steely grey eyes, he added, 'I think, General, that you may be able to tell us a thing or two. I could not help but notice that last night Mrs Williams came out of the same bedroom as you.'

'Excuse me for interrupting, but we can't leave a dead body lying in the bath,' said the maid. It was she who had discovered Mrs Williams as she had been about to run Miss Fry's bathwater. She seemed to have recovered from the initial shock and now appeared to be excited by the event rather than distraught. This was understandable since it was not every day that a maid found a dead body in the bath. 'If you don't mind me saying so, I do think that this is very exciting! It's like a detective book or one of those films you see at the picture house. I hope that you don't think me gruesome to be talking this way.'

'No, no of course not,' Reverend Peters assured the girl. 'It's quite understandable that you should feel that way; I know that I did when I saw my first dead body.'

'Was that a vampire victim?' enquired Miss Fry.

'No. It was at a funeral,' he answered casually. 'It was

a very big day for me, the very first funeral that I ever conducted all by myself.'

'How clever of you,' murmured Miss Fry. She had a feeling that the conversation was verging on bad taste.

'I see what you mean about the body though,' Reverend Peters continued. 'It's not the sort of thing one can leave hanging around . . . or should I say floating around?' Everyone except for General Habinger laughed politely at the little joke. 'We had better take the body out of the bath because the water will disfigure the body and we don't want to stain the bath with that blue dye more than we can help, do we?'

There was a dull thud as the General fainted. Pierre du Bois, who appeared to be very knowledgeable about these things, turned him over and put him into the recovery position.

'He seems quite distressed at Mrs Williams having passed away,' observed Pierre.

'Perhaps I should offer him some religious consolation when he comes round,' Reverend Peters suggested. 'Or maybe I could do a reading from the Bible.'

'All in good time,' Pierre said. He turned to the maid who seemed willing to please. 'There is another body further down the hall . . .'

'My, my!' exclaimed the maid. 'Another! We have been busy, haven't we?'

'Yes, indeed,' Pierre said quickly, slightly annoyed at having been interrupted while issuing instructions. 'I would like you to get the porter and the butler to help you take that body and this one and lay them both out on the dining-room table. Then come straight to the drawing room where we will discuss the best course of action.'

'By Golly!' exclaimed Miss Fry. 'That young girl, Joan Summers, is still locked inside the drawing room.'

'She might not be in there,' Reverend Peters said

thoughtfully. 'If she murdered Edmund and we find that she has escaped from the drawing room, I think that we can assume that she drowned Mrs Williams.'

The maid had been standing nearby, listening agog, but when Pierre cast her an irritated glance she went off, with regret, to find the butler and porter. The General, who was just beginning to come round, was carried down the hall to the drawing room. Joan was banging the door with her fists trying to get attention.

'What's going on out there?' she cried.

Miss Fry turned the key in the lock and pushed the door open. Pierre and the vicar put the General on the sofa.

'Is he dead?' Joan asked with a certain amount of hope in her voice. 'Thanks to him I spent the night on an extremely lumpy sofa, and the lumps were in all the most awkward places.'

'No, he isn't dead,' said Miss Fry. She moved the General's feet off the sofa and sat down. As he weakly opened his eyes she gave his cheeks a couple of slaps, because this was what the heroes always did in books.

'Here you are, General,' Reverend Peters said as he handed the recovering man a drink.

'Madame Summers, I must ask where you were last night,' Pierre said sternly.

'Where on earth do you think I was?' Joan said crossly. 'In here of course. Where else could I have been? I was locked in, in case you've forgotten.'

'I had not forgotten,' Pierre said. 'Early this morning another murder was committed.'

'Really . . . Who?' asked Joan.

'Mrs Williams,' came the reply. Pierre, unlike the others, was fully dressed, and wearing the same clothes he had worn the previous day, complete with the string of onions. Miss Fry noticing the onions and remembering her allergy, moved herself further away to an armchair.

'Mrs Williams?' questioned Joan. She was screwing up her forehead as she tried to recall. 'Oh I remember, the woman with the blue hair.'

'Or rather the not so very blue hair now,' Miss Fry muttered to herself.

'I think,' said Reverend Peters, who rarely thought, 'that we can come to the assumption that young Joan could not possibly have escaped from this room and drowned Mrs Williams.'

'Drowned? But there's no lake or river near Waddington,' Joan said.

'She was drowned in the bath,' Reverend Peters said with a melancholy sigh. 'God rest her soul. I do wish that there had been time for me to hear a confession from her.'

'But you're not a Catholic priest,' said Pierre.

'No, I'm just a jolly old C of E, but confessions are frightfully interesting to hear; in fact they are probably the only excitement we vicars get.'

'Drowned in her bath,' murmured Joan, looking pale. 'What a quaint way to go.'

'So it appears that we have not one but two murderers in our midst,' Reverend Peters said, looking at the others with eagle eyes as though trying to guess who was guilty. 'What a den of thieves this is.'

'Don't you mean den of murderers?' questioned Miss Fry, though when she thought about it, she could not remember having seen the expression in her book of quotations.

'Yes, I suppose I do, but one does usually talk about a den of thieves rather than of murderers,' he replied, looking slightly crestfallen at having been corrected by Miss Fry. He was not used to being corrected by anyone; this was the result of an Eton education and having an archbishop for a father.

'Look,' said Joan, abruptly, 'although Edmund and

I had our differences last night, I most certainly did not murder him. So, you might now be looking for one murderer still, or maybe two, but either way I'm innocent.'

'Rubbish!' exclaimed General Habinger, who had now fully recovered and seemed to be none the worse for his faint. Falling flat on his face had cracked his monocle and as he had not noticed it no one else could be bothered to take the trouble to point it out. 'The evidence was all against you last night, and there's no way you can deny it.'

'How dare you insinuate that I'm guilty when I'm innocent until proven otherwise in a court of law!' Joan shouted angrily. She had her eyes fixed on a Chinese vase standing on the coffee table and she looked as though she would dearly like to smash it over the General's head.

'Madame Summers,' Pierre began. 'If my memory is correct, I believe that when the General locked you in this room last night, you shouted – or perhaps screamed would be a more apt word – that all of us had motives to kill your husband. Well?'

'I was just coming to that,' said Joan in a self-satisfied voice and with a smug smile. 'As Edmund told you at dinner he is, or was, a journalist. But he was not a reporter for just any old national newspaper, but for *Slanderous Daily*!'

'No!' cried the others in a hushed, shocked chorus. They now knew what kind of newspaper Edmund had worked for. This paper was dreaded by every eminent celebrity, be they actor, royalty or bishop. They called themselves slanderous, but they were not so in the strict legal sense, since every story reported was true but with just the right amount of modification. If anyone in the public eye lived a double life with sordid secrets, it would be discovered by the journalists, using fair means and foul, mainly the latter. Everyone who was anyone lived in fear of being exposed by the *Slanderous Daily*.

'Yes,' said Joan with obvious pride and relish. 'He was their star reporter and I was his secretary.'

'This leaves you unemployed then,' Miss Fry said with a giggle. At times she could not stop herself laughing at other people's misfortunes. 'But why does this information now make us suspects?'

'I'm sorry to disappoint you, Reverend, but Edmund never wrote a scrap of poetry in his life,' said Joan continuing with her startling revelations.

'Oh,' said the startled vicar. 'Not one?'

'No, I'm afraid not,' said Joan. 'He wasn't the sort.'

'But how strange, I was so sure, and I'm usually right about these things,' said Reverend Peters sounding a little sad. 'But what was he writing down all the time in his little notebook?'

'He was writing notes for an article, an article on all of you. It was going to be a scorcher, a real shocker; it would have been the crowning article of his career – if someone hadn't crowned him first. He was going to write about the dark secrets of the average New Year guest at Waddington Castle. One of you could have realized who he was, since we didn't come incognito, and killed him to keep him quiet.' Joan sat back and watched with obvious pleasure as the others squirmed.

'What would any of us have to hide?' General Habinger bluffed angrily.

'You tell me. Edmund had already discovered a number of interesting things about you. Like that you and Mrs Williams came here together, instead of Mrs Williams being at her sick sister's house which is where she told her husband she would be. Goodness knows how her death at Waddington Castle will be explained to her husband. As for the rest of you, I can't say exactly what Edmund found out about you because someone has stolen his note-book.'

Miss Fry sighed with relief. She had no wish to have her gypsy ancestry and love for historical romances revealed in a national newspaper: what would the Women's Institute say? Edmund's newspaper was the only one they read and they were in fact addicted to it. 'Daddy would turn in his grave if he knew,' she thought. 'At least he would if his ashes weren't scattered over Lake Windermere.'

There came a knock at the door and the butler, maid and porter came into the drawing room. Without being invited they helped themselves to drinks and sat down. 'Well,' said Pierre du Bois to the butler. He was chewing one end of his moustache thoughtfully. 'Did you move the bodies?'

'Yes . . . sir,' answered the butler. He found it difficult to address a foreigner as 'sir', and a Frenchman at that. He was a tall man with white hair and he looked every inch an English gentleman's butler. Since the departure of his previous employer, Sir Horace Hedgeworthy, for the Bahamas, he had not enjoyed his work; he knew that he would never get used to the steady stream of different guests taking up residence at Waddington Castle every couple of weeks.

'That must have been a horrible job,' commented Joan. Having led a very sheltered life she had never had the task of helping to carry a dead body and found it difficult to imagine. She soon lost her macabre interest though when she remembered that one of the bodies belonged to her late husband. She hoped that the management would not charge her for the bloodstained white carpet.

'It was indeed a nasty job,' agreed the butler. 'But one has to get used to these things, Miss. Of course it isn't normally my job, but the gardeners go home early every evening at this time of year and of course they'll use the snow as an excuse for not coming in this morning.'

'It all seems very obvious to me,' said Miss Fry, who was beginning to feel left out. 'I expect the butler did it!'

'That would be just a little too obvious,' said the maid bad-temperedly. She did not like Miss Fry very much, but thought that the butler was rather handsome.

'Oh, I almost forgot,' said the butler, reaching in his jacket pocket. 'We found this in the bathwater after we took the body out.'

General Habinger groaned, went very pale and looked as though he might faint again.

The butler held out a medal with a soggy crimson ribbon. Reverend Peters took it from him.

'I say, a medal!' he exclaimed brightly. 'Just like the one I noticed General Habinger wearing last night on his uniform. What an amazing coincidence that there should be two identical medals in one castle . . .' He stopped abruptly when he noticed that everyone was staring at him.

General Habinger's face had become beetroot red and he sank lower down in his chair as all the room turned their attention to him. He tried to speak but was so shocked at the discovery of the medal that he was unable to say a word.

'So you did it!' hissed Joan. 'That was why you were so anxious to put the blame on me for killing Edmund and have me locked up in here because it was you who did it all along! You killed both of them!'

'Oh, General Habinger isn't guilty,' Miss Fry blurted out.

'How should you know?' asked Pierre du Bois sharply.

'I just have a feeling,' replied Miss Fry. 'Inside of me I can feel that he didn't.'

'Oh yes he did!' shouted Joan, jumping to her feet. 'He killed my darling Edmund, the best husband any woman could hope to have.' Edmund's brutal death was obviously making Joan forget what a rotten cad he had really been. She made her way over to the General and glaring menacingly she put her hands round his throat. General Habinger started to make strange gurgling noises, rolling his eyes around expressively, when the others suddenly realized that Joan was trying to kill him. Pierre du Bois and Reverend Peters pulled her off.

'I think that rather proves the young lady's guilt,' commented the butler.

'Shut up!' chorused everyone.

'I wish that I could be allowed to explain myself,' protested General Habinger who was beginning to feel that the battle was not going his way.

'Go on, Monsieur, but it had better be good,' said Pierre.

'I . . . I . . .' General Habinger was highly embarrassed at what he was about to admit. 'I gave Mrs Williams the medal as . . . as a gift.'

'A gift!' exclaimed Joan in disbelief. Had Edmund given her a present as mundane as a medal she would have hit him.

'Yes . . . er . . . as a token of my affection,' said General Habinger.

'Oh,' chorused everyone, at last understanding his meaning – though no one could make up their minds whether they believed him or not.

'The thing is,' Reverend Peters said, 'what are we going to do? We can't telephone the police to inform them about what has been going on here, because the lines are down.'

'We have to contact the police,' said General Habinger, back to his bossy old self now he felt the medal business was explained. He got up from the sofa and went and stood by the window. 'Weather conditions are diabolical,' he informed the others. 'We'd never be able to drive a car out of here.'

Pierre du Bois walked over to join him. 'Perhaps one of us could make it to the village on foot,' he suggested.

'I'm willing to go,' said the butler. 'And the boy will accompany me,' he continued, gesturing to the porter who looked less than keen.

'That's very sporting of you both,' said Reverend Peters. 'But isn't it liable to be a bit dangerous?'

'Nonsense! They'll be as right as rain, or should I say right as snow? Why I've been on army manoeuvres in worse conditions than this,' said the General. 'I would come along with you if I were only a few years younger.'

'I bet you would,' muttered Joan.

'Well then, we will both be off then,' said the butler. He took a firm hold of the porter's wrist and opened the drawing-room door. The unfortunate porter looked as though he was on the verge of tears or running away, possibly both.

There was silence in the room as the two men left. The only noise and movement was that of the steady ticking of the grandfather clock.

'Will you all be wanting breakfast now?' asked the maid. She did not expect anyone to take up her offer. In the films she'd seen people seldom felt up to eating breakfast after a murder had been committed in the vicinity, though usually they had recovered by lunch time.

'Oh good show!' cried General Habinger. 'I'm simply ravenous.'

'Me too,' agreed Miss Fry.

'Oh . . .' said the maid, who was now wondering if the films had been right after all. 'What would you like? It might take a little while to cook because there's only me to do it. We usually have a woman from the village who comes in every day, but of course she can't in this weather. She telephoned last night before the lines came down to say she wouldn't be here.'

'I would like a continental breakfast please,' said Miss Fry. She had acquired this taste from her adventurous expedition to France.

'I'll have a proper English breakfast, none of that foreign muck for me,' said the General. He looked sternly at Miss Fry, whom he had previously thought to be a good patriotic Englishwoman. 'I'll have bacon and eggs, toast with plenty of honey and a glass of port,' he continued.

'I will have onion soup,' Pierre said as he handed the astonished maid two onions. 'I never start the day off without a good onion from my homeland. My mother makes the best onion soup in the world.'

'Well if you don't think that it comes up to standard here, you can go back to her,' Joan suggested rudely. She seemed nervous and agitated as she added a new coat of pink varnish to her fingernails and she was visibly shaking.

'And what would you like, Reverend?' asked the maid. She was obviously not the average semi-literate maid as she was writing down all of the orders in neat copperplate.

'I'll be a bit of a devil and have several crumpets dripping with honey and butter,' Reverend Peters replied, his mouth watering at the very thought of it. 'After we've eaten, as a special treat, I'll read some psalms and parables.'

'How exciting,' Miss Fry commented with a certain lack of enthusiasm. Psalm and parable reading in her experience was not a bundle of laughs.

'I can't believe the way you're all acting,' said Joan. She was wringing her hands, but with care so as not to damage her carefully painted nails. 'This is an absolute nightmare that we're living through, yet all you can discuss is what to have for breakfast!'

'A nightmare?' asked Reverend Peters. 'I hadn't noticed. Compared with my little brush with a hamlet of vampires this is heaven – well, almost!'

Chapter Six

iss Fry was in love! For the first time in her life she had met what she considered to be a 'real man'.

She had started to succumb to General Habinger's charms at dinner the previous evening. She had felt a brief fluttering of butterflies in her stomach but had at first put it down to the prawns. And yet she had not felt quite like that since she had had a mild crush on a French teacher when she was a young schoolgirl.

Miss Fry was quite an observant woman and had noticed Mrs Williams's adoring and intimate glances at the General. At first she had put these looks down to admiration as the two had not said that they were close acquaintances. Miss Fry had found herself sending looks of a similar nature to the General, though quite unconsciously. A real lady would never do such a thing knowingly. As the night had worn on, Miss Fry had come to realize that they did indeed know each other and that they had obviously come to Waddington Castle without the knowledge of Mr Williams. After Edmund's murder when everyone had rushed out of their bedrooms, Miss Fry had been quite devastated when she saw General Habinger come out of the same bedroom as Mrs Williams. Miss Fry had thought this very scandalous but she still could not help feeling envious and wishing herself in Mrs Williams's position. It was with great sadness that Miss Fry had realized that there was no hope for her as another woman had got there first.

In General Habinger, Miss Fry was able to find everything that she wanted in a man. He was obviously brave, well paid and he had a monocle. She had always had a weakness for men with monocles! He had a firm jutting chin, which Miss Fry found herself doodling on a notepad on her dressing table. Now that Mrs Williams was dead, Miss Fry could not help but wonder if she had a chance. General Habinger obviously liked good food and Miss Fry's gingerbread and sticky buns had been the best in Penton and had always sold well at the village fête. And did people not say that the way to a man's heart was through his stomach? Miss Fry made a mental note to go and look at the kitchens to see if the correct ingredients for gingerbread and sticky buns were available.

The only thing that Miss Fry could find to dislike about the General were his remarks about women who drank alcohol. 'He might think me a fallen woman,' she thought miserably. 'But when I get him to marry me I can drink in secret, and even if he did find out he could hardly divorce me on the grounds of being unladylike, could he?' She also wondered about Mrs Williams's blue hair. 'I do hope that the General didn't ask her to dye it that ghastly colour. I'm sure that his tastes are much better and more conservative, but one can never tell; he might have a passion for women with light-blue hair. Well, if he really wanted me to have blue hair, I suppose I wouldn't mind too much.'

Miss Fry quickly changed into a tweed jacket and skirt. To add a suitably feminine touch she put a dab of perfume called 'Lethal' behind each ear. After reading three pages of her novel, Miss Fry felt too bored and distracted to continue. The heroine in the book was just being carried off by an Arabian knight: she could picture the image clearly in her mind, but the Arabian had become General Habinger and the heroine herself. This had a certain lack of realism since the General was quite short in stature and she had a feeling that he would not be capable of carrying her off even if he wanted to.

'I wonder what his Christian name is,' Miss Fry said aloud, with a faraway dreamy look in her eyes. 'Probably something incredibly masculine like Reginald or Horatio or, better still, Heathcliff.'

Miss Fry picked up a piece of paper and with a pencil scribbled 'Esmerelda Fry, Esmerelda Habinger, Mrs Habinger.' She liked the last one best of all. Screwing the paper up into a ball, she threw it at the wastepaper basket. It did not go in, and Miss Fry who was becoming notoriously lazy now that her father had gone, could not be bothered to pick it up.

She was feeling decidedly bored now. Although she was used to the quiet life, she had in the last twenty-four hours had her first taste of freedom, the high life, murder, mystery and mayhem, so the present silence seemed an anti-climax if not plain dull. There was at least half an hour before breakfast would be ready and nothing to do in it. As she looked around the bedroom, in the various empty drawers and cupboards, she wondered why hotel rooms even in castles had such an impersonal feel to them. She considered whether she should write a letter to the proprietor suggesting that a more homely atmosphere would be better in these surroundings.

'Oh botheration!' she suddenly cursed. 'I completely forgot to ask the maid to make some hot drinking-chocolate for me: how can I possibly enjoy breakfast without any?

73

Perhaps in a few minutes I'll go and see if I can find where the kitchens are and ask for some; and while I'm at it I can look at the available cake ingredients.' She paused: 'But I've one or two other things to attend to before I go and do that . . .'

Joan Summers had also changed very quickly into more suitable clothes, but she was not bored or at a loss as to what she should do. First she touched up her hair roots which to her horror had been growing out the golden peroxide dye. She was a young woman of about twenty. She was also very pretty in a flashy sort of way, and looked a little like the Hollywood film star Jean Harlow. She had an educated voice with a distinctly upper-class accent, though this was by training rather than by birth.

'What would Edmund do if he were here?' she said aloud. Her husband had reported on several murder investigations and had considered himself to be quite an expert on amateur detection. 'I think that the first thing to do is to snoop around the castle. Perhaps the murderer isn't one of the guests and is hiding somewhere and planning to murder us one by one while watching us accuse and suspect each other.'

Feeling very frightened and not at all brave, Joan left her bedroom determined to search for the dastardly villain who was not killing by the rules. When she came to the end of the corridor and on to the landing, she wondered whether she should go upstairs or downstairs first. She decided that upstairs would be the most likely, though she felt a little wary as she was afraid that she might be followed up or pushed down the stairs.

'I say!' she exclaimed, silently, because she knew that it was not particularly wise to speak to oneself out loud while a murderer was hanging around. Her attention had been caught by an axe that was hanging on the wall ten steps up. It was identical to the one implanted in Edmund's back. There was a faint line where the one used to kill Edmund must once have hung, making a cross with the axe that remained.

Joan, who had not been married to a reporter for nothing, realized that the murderer had been this way, so she ran lightly up the flight of forty carpeted stairs until she came to the second floor. The corridor was in darkness, so she fumbled around on the wall looking for a light switch. She could not help wondering if perhaps there was someone in the darkness with her, someone who would grab her at any moment. When she eventually did find the light switch she was almost too afraid to press it, for fear of what she might see. Once she had plucked up enough courage she was relieved to see that there was no one there. It appeared to be just a corridor of empty bedrooms, much the same as the floor below. Still, she reasoned, no stone should be left unturned. So she bravely opened each door and went inside. The furniture in each bedroom was covered with white sheets, which at first scared the living daylights out of her because she had thought them to be ghosts, about which she had a phobia. However she dutifully looked under each sheet, each bed and into each wardrobe and cupboard.

After a row of ten equally boring bedrooms she came to the bathroom, a place she could not bring herself to investigate because of Mrs Williams's misadventure: she was understandably anxious to avoid the same fate. As she walked along, she had the curious feeling that she was being followed. Joan repeatedly turned round quickly to see if anyone was there but either she was too slow or the follower was too fast: she could see no one. She realized that it had been a mistake to wear high-heeled shoes, for however quietly she tried to walk, they still went clip-clop. As well as the noise there was also the chance, if she met the murderer, that she would have to run for her life, and she realized that her shoes were hardly suitable for the purpose. So she slipped them off and put them neatly beside the wall. One could hardly leave them just anywhere as someone might trip over them, she thought.

This part of the castle was, to put it mildly, tatty, compared with the floor below. There were cobwebs everywhere, some going from one wall of the corridor to the other. Every time Joan broke through the tanglement of white thread she shuddered as though she had just heard the grating of a piece of chalk being scratched across a blackboard. She had had a tremendous fear of spiders ever since she was a little girl. The sight of one sitting in the bath was enough to send her into hysterical screams. To stop herself from screaming now she was exercising such strict self-control that she had never realized that she possessed it. Joan could not help but wonder as she brushed through each web if perhaps a spider seeing that its home was being destroyed had jumped for refuge on to her back or head. As soon as these terrifying thoughts came to mind she was sure that she could feel the dainty feet of at least sixteen huge, black, hairy-legged spiders, all in different places. She was, however, too afraid to put her hands on to her back and head to see if they were present or not, and so she continued, shuddering every time she thought that she felt the hideous creatures, though where she was going she had no idea.

'If only there were signposts!' she thought miserably. Not for the first time, and not the last time either, she wished that she and Edmund had never come, though she realized that Edmund's timely death had saved her from a scandalous divorce, and instead left her a respectable widow. 'Sometimes I wonder if I would have been happier as a flower girl at Covent Garden . . .'

At the end of the corridor there was a large, rectangular-shaped door. It was locked. Joan tugged at it determinedly before realizing the obvious. Having been a Brownie and a Girl Guide (invaluable training for a life of action and adventure) she had always learnt to 'be prepared'. Today was no exception, since she had in her golden hair a pin that was ideal for picking the locks of old rectangular-shaped doors in castles.

Within two minutes Joan had the door open. It hadn't occurred to her that if the door was locked it was perhaps unlikely that the fiendish, dastardly murderer was hiding behind it. But still, perhaps Joan had more brains than met the eye and had cleverly picked the lock because she realized that the murderer could have locked himself behind the door in order to hide.

Behind the large, rectangular-shaped door was another door. This time much smaller, so small that Joan would have to bend double to get through it. It reminded Joan of *Alice in Wonderland* and she half expected to see a table with a bottle on it with a label saying 'drink me'. This door was also locked, but Joan, with increased enthusiasm, had it open even quicker than the first. She began to feel a little annoyed when behind this door was another, this time even smaller. Joan was reminded of her eighth birthday when she had received a gigantic parcel inside which were smaller and smaller cardboard boxes and eventually a very small gift: everyone had thought it very amusing, except Joan.

This door was not locked so Joan opened it. To get through she had to crawl on hands and knees. Once through, she found herself at the foot of a flight of tiny stone stairs. They obviously led up to a tower because the staircase ascended in a tight spiral. Joan very cautiously started to go up. There was no handrail so she stepped up sideways with her back to the wall. It was very awkward, for she could only see what was ahead for a few steps because of the way the staircase wound round. Although there was no electric light, Joan could see perfectly because there were several small windows, but she could not see much outside as these were so narrow and so deep. It was very cold, probably because of the snow but stone steps and walls did not exactly help matters.

For the first time Joan wished that she had a gun. She had no idea how to use one but she had seen plenty of films at the cinema, and it never looked too difficult. 'I bet General Habinger's got a gun,' she thought grudgingly. 'I can't see someone like him going anywhere without one. That could rule him out as the murderer: surely if he was he would have shot Edmund and Mrs Williams . . . but that would be all too obvious, wouldn't it? Still,' she pondered, 'if he was a psychopath it would be impossible to reason his motives and actions . . .

'And what about the others? It's all so difficult. What about Miss Fry? She seems harmless enough and I can't see her chopping someone up with an axe, or drowning someone in a bath: all the same one can never tell with old ladies . . .

'Reverend Peters seems a nice man, not too pious, thank God! It could be him; those terrifying experiences with vampires could so easily have unhinged him. And the Frenchman . . . what was his name? . . . Pierre something or other. I think that it's him. He looks like a psychopathic murderer to me. Whoever heard of an onion seller wearing onions round his neck all day long?

'Lastly there's the castle employees – the maid, porter and butler. The porter and butler seemed far too enthusiastic about hiking to the village. It's quite possible that they didn't go, and are up here and hiding – and are planning to murder us one by one!'

At the top of the stairs was an arch-shaped heavy wooden door. Joan looked round nervously to check that no one was behind her, and then turned the brass key in the lock. Joan went into the room, her heart in her mouth. It was a large room, in the shape of a circle. No sooner had she gone in than she heard footsteps running up the stone staircase. Joan stood rooted to the spot, too afraid to move. She was certain that at any moment she was going to have her throat cut. What was she to do? Where could she go? She shut her eyes – it seemed the most sensible thing to do. There was a bang, a jangle, and the sound of running footsteps going down. Joan opened one eye, then the other. She was alone.

When her heart had left her mouth and had stopped pounding she ran over to the door. She tugged at the handle – so hard that it came off in her hands. The door was locked and no amount of picking would unlock it. Joan was alone with nothing to do, except feel sorry for herself, something which she was very good at.

Chapter Seven

At the appointed time General Habinger, Pierre du Bois, Miss Fry and Reverend Peters were sitting in the drawing room, feeling very sorry for themselves as breakfast had not yet arrived. They had unanimously decided to eat in the drawing room in preference to the dining room – it would have been very macabre as the two bodies were laid out on the table.

'Where is that damn girl?' complained General Habinger. 'How can a man be expected to start the day without a good, solid breakfast inside him?'

'Goodness!' exclaimed Miss Fry, with a startled gasp. 'Do you realize that today is the very last day of nineteen thirty-six?'

'So it is,' agreed Reverend Peters. 'All this excitement had made me quite forget. I must admit that I will be glad to get on with nineteen thirty-seven. This has not been a very good year for me, as you have no doubt guessed.'

'Indeed,' clucked Miss Fry sympathetically. 'You certainly do deserve some luck.'

Pierre du Bois nibbled at a raw onion. He was now very hungry and his opinion of British hotel service was not good.

'Well we can hardly blame the poor girl,' said Miss Fry charitably. 'Such a lot of work for one person . . . do you suppose that I should go down to the kitchens to see if I can possibly help her out?'

'Certainly not!' General Habinger said firmly. 'You do not pay bills – and expensive ones at that – to have to do your own cooking.'

So that was that. They sat quietly, as there was no conversation to make, for a good twenty-five minutes, but no breakfast in any shape or form appeared. General Habinger was beginning to regret his hasty words, wishing that he had let Miss Fry go and do his breakfast.

'I say, this is a jolly bad show,' commented Reverend Peters. He did not like to be critical, but on this occasion felt quite justified.

'In France breakfast is always on time, even if the gardener has to prepare it,' Pierre du Bois remarked solemnly.

'Where do you suppose Mrs Summers has got to?' asked Miss Fry, with concern. 'I do hope that she is quite all right.'

'I daresay that she's shut herself in her bedroom and is sulking, crying, or most likely both,' General Habinger answered, with a noticeable lack of sympathy. 'Silly girl, getting distraught over nothing.'

'Hardly over nothing,' interrupted Pierre du Bois. 'Remember her husband was murdered . . .' he looked around at the others with eagle eyes, 'by one of us.'

'Nonsense!' General Habinger argued indignantly. 'I stick by my original theory that she murdered that young man herself. I believe that she is a clever, vindictive young woman who will stop at nothing to get what she wants and who will push anyone out of the way who tries to stop her.'

'And Mrs Williams?' Pierre du Bois questioned. 'Do you

81

believe that the Summers girl also murdered her? What would her motive have been?'

'I don't wish to discuss that!' General Habinger snapped with such finality in his voice that no one dared to pursue the point.

'I say, this is a jolly bad show,' repeated Reverend Peters, forgetting that he had said exactly the same thing only minutes earlier.

Miss Fry gave him one of her fiercest irritated looks. 'What an odious little man,' she thought. 'I feel like telling him so too, but that wouldn't be ladylike.' She felt so bored that she felt like screaming; anything to break this fearful monotony.

'I think that we should all go to the kitchens and find out what is holding up my breakfast – I mean our breakfast,' said General Habinger. It was not a suggestion, but an order, with the implication that if anyone dared not follow it they would be shot. He would not have known how to make a suggestion even if he had wanted to.

'I agree,' said Pierre du Bois. 'I am famished.' He was beginning to chew another onion, which he knew was not the wisest of actions as how was an onion seller to sell onions if he had eaten them all?

General Habinger began to lead the way, as he was accustomed to doing, even though he did not have the remotest idea in which direction the kitchens lay. He marched along rapidly, with Pierre du Bois close behind; Miss Fry, who was trailing at the back, had to run to keep up.

'Excuse me,' said Miss Fry timidly. Being madly in love with General Habinger she had no wish to wound his manly pride, but she felt it her duty to inform him, 'But you are going in the wrong direction.'

'How would you know where the kitchens are?' rapped

General Habinger with bad grace. As he did not know that Miss Fry was madly in love with him, he was just as rude to her as he was to everyone else.

'Woman's intuition?' Miss Fry suggested lightly, blushing furiously and with a soppy grin on her small face.

'Well, where do you think they are, Miss Fry?' he asked nastily. He had a vibrant note of sarcasm in his voice. He hated to be told that he was wrong by anyone, but a woman was the lowest of the low, and therefore could not know better than he!

'A kitchen would never be in the guest wing. The logical place to look is in the basement, so I suggest that we go and investigate that quarter right away,' said Miss Fry brightly.

'Hum . . .' snorted General Habinger, sounding rather like a camel. 'I suppose there's no harm in trying.'

'Oh, how masterful he is!' she thought breathlessly. She was not insulted by General Habinger's rude remarks, far from it. It corresponded with her image of the ideal man. All of the heroes in her historical romance novels had a sardonic sense of humour, and she mistook General Habinger's rude behaviour for the very quality for which she was searching. 'If only he and I were alone together, just the two of us on the sands of a sensuous desert island eating my homemade gingerbread and drinking coconut milk!' she thought. 'We would be so happy together, so free.'

'That seems a sensible enough idea,' commented Reverend Peters, breaking Miss Fry's reverie.

Miss Fry led the way, at a sensible pace, down the main stairs, along a rather tatty passage, on through a door and down another flight of stairs into the kitchens, a feat accomplished with such ease it was almost as if she had been that way before.

'Your woman's instinct serves you well,' said Pierre du

Bois. 'How remarkable that you should find it so easily, first time without any mistakes.'

Miss Fry chose to remain silent. She had always found it difficult, even as a child, to think of quick, witty – not to mention rude – replies to such patronizing remarks.

The kitchens were very large, and not at all homely; instead they were cold and unfriendly, just as one would expect to find a castle kitchen. It was rather like a school kitchen – dirty and smelly, with huge saucepans on massive stoves containing unidentifiable substances, all of which looked quite uneatable.

General Habinger with his usual air of command and authority walked ahead of the others at a fast trot, all of a sudden stopping dead . . . not literally speaking, of course.

'What is it?' asked Miss Fry, running swiftly to his side. She had found herself about to call General Habinger 'darling' and had only just stopped herself in time. 'He doesn't know how I feel about him,' she remembered sadly. 'Or maybe he does – surely a man with his perception and sensitivity can't be blind to these electric currents between us; I can feel them flying through the air!'

Within moments the others were at their side. No one needed to answer Miss Fry's question, as the truth was plain to see. Lying at the foot of the cooker was the maid; her mouth was open wide, making her look very silly.

'Is she drunk?' asked Miss Fry, with surprising naivety. Having often passed out at the foot of her cooker after one drink too many she thought it reasonable to suggest that the same thing might have happened to the maid while cooking breakfast.

'What are you, a halfwit?' General Habinger snapped, seizing the girl's wrist to take her pulse. 'She's dead.' Miss Fry was beginning to suspect that perhaps her first great love's remarks were not due to a sardonic sense of humour but the result instead of downright rudeness. But, she tried to tell herself, General Habinger was a very clever man and perhaps it was this tremendous pressure that was causing his childish behaviour.

'How did she die?' Reverend Peters asked with enthusiasm.

'I'm not sure,' murmured General Habinger, almost inaudibly. He did not like having to admit that there was something that he did not know.

'Have a look at her neck,' Reverend Peters suggested helpfully. 'If there are two little slits they could be vampire bites, which means we'll have to perform certain bloody rituals to the body to prevent the maid rising as another vampire.'

'No, there are no marks,' General Habinger stated as soon as he had checked. He sounded faintly disappointed as he had never seen vampire bites before and was always interested in different modes of death. He would probably have enjoyed performing those certain bloody rites too.

Pierre du Bois, being a practical sort of chap who did not believe in vampires, started to examine the scene of the crime; assuming that a crime had actually been committed.

'It is possible that it was not a murder,' Miss Fry said. 'There's no sign of a struggle; perhaps it was a heart attack or something.'

'It could have been suicide,' Reverend Peters considered. 'The unfortunate girl, seeing all these things, could have gone out of her mind and ended it all.'

'I hardly think so,' said Miss Fry. 'On the contrary, she seemed to be getting a sort of schoolgirl excitement out of it.'

'Well if you don't think that it was murder and you don't think that it was suicide, what do you think it was?' General Habinger asked, bad temperedly. He considered

Miss Fry to be the most irritatingly stupid woman it had ever been his misfortune to meet.

'Heart failure?' Miss Fry suggested weakly.

General Habinger raised his eyes to the ceiling muttering, 'Give me strength.'

Pierre du Bois seemed to be a more than averagely intelligent onion seller, since he produced from his red-trouser pockets a large magnifying glass with which he began to examine the top of the cooker and surrounding work surface. The half-prepared breakfast was on a table and a small jar with a pipette was beside it. The jar was filled a quarter of the way up with a reddish brown liquid.

'What do you suppose this is?' asked Reverend Peters, as he picked up the little jar and sniffed its suspect contents. 'It looks like nose drops.'

'Having never used nose drops, I wouldn't know,' General Habinger said shortly. He was very, very hungry and when in that nervous condition he always became extremely irritable, grunting and groaning like a bear with a sore head until he got something inside him. He knew from vast experience that men marched on their stomachs.

Miss Fry took an apple with rosy cheeks from a nearby fruit bowl and having first carefully polished it on the hem of her skirt, took a large bite. 'Oh!' she exclaimed loudly, with a touch of melodrama.

'What is it?' asked Reverend Peters with concern. 'It isn't poisoned is it?'

'Oh no,' Miss Fry answered reassuringly. 'I gasped with pleasure; this is quite the nicest apple I've had since I went scrumping as a young girl.'

Pierre du Bois having finished his examination of the cooker, took the bottle from Reverend Peters and sniffed it appreciatively. After having held it up to the light and sniffed it several more times, he put it back on the table.

'I believe that the liquid inside that bottle is without

any doubt – cyanide.' Pierre du Bois sounded a little smug, but that was understandable since he had proposed this astounding theorem before the others.

'Rubbish!' General Habinger said loudly. 'What would poison be doing in a kitchen . . . as if an onion seller would know the difference between soy sauce and cyanide, and a foreigner at that.'

'If you don't believe me why don't you sample it,' suggested Pierre lightly. He held out the bottle. Although he appeared to be a mild-natured man, his blood was steadily rising to boiling point. He was beginning to hate General Habinger and considered him to be a dastardly brute. How dare this man insult his beloved country France! How dare he insult the noble trade of onion selling! Pierre du Bois comforted himself with the thought that the General would not be so flippant if he knew the truth about him.

General Habinger snatched the bottle from Pierre's hand but looked a little uncertain about whether he should drink some or not. He decided to do so, telling himself that his own and England's honour was at stake. Where he acquired this strange notion can only be guessed at. Miss Fry had been watching these proceedings with a look of growing horror. Just as General Habinger was about to put the bottle to his lips, Miss Fry knocked it from his hand from where it fell to the stone floor, smashing into several thousand pieces.

The others stared at Miss Fry in amazement. They had previously thought of her as a frail old lady; they had heard of mice turning into tigers, but . . . Miss Fry looked as surprised as they. She had hardly thought about what she was doing, it was almost as though the action had been done by reflex.

'I'm so . . . so sorry, I don't know what came over me,' she stammered. The first part was a lie, she was not at all sorry for what she had done, and was willing to do anything else to save her beloved idol.

'Hum . . .' muttered General Habinger. Surprisingly enough he was not ranting and raving and seemed to be as struck dumb as Miss Fry was.

'Oh dear,' murmured Miss Fry. She could not think of anything more intelligent to say.

'That's quite all right, my dear,' General Habinger said, coughing slightly with embarrassment. He patted Miss Fry gingerly on the shoulder. 'It wasn't your fault.' He turned angrily to look at Pierre du Bois. 'I blame that damn foreign fool, must have scared the living daylights out of you.'

Miss Fry was almost swooning with pleasure. How noble General Habinger was, and oh so brave! She had heard only his first few words; after he had called her 'dear' her mind had emptied. Pierre du Bois could not help but notice this, as he was an observant type of man, and wondered about it.

'If it was poison, were we the intended victims?' asked Reverend Peters, realization dawning.

'By Jove!' shouted General Habinger, jumping with excitement. 'I can see it all now, the little blighters were trying to poison me.'

'What little blighters . . . dear?' asked Miss Fry. She wondered if the nervously added endearment was perhaps a little too presumptuous, but General Habinger seemed not to have noticed, or if he had noticed he obviously did not object.

'Foreigners!' he exclaimed, now in his element. 'The Germans of course!'

'And the French?' Pierre asked sarcastically.

'I see, German little blighters,' humoured Reverend Peters.

'Well it's no more ridiculous than you and your damn

vampires!' General Habinger snapped. He was now pacing up and down. 'Those German spies want me out of the way.'

'Why would German spies want you out of the way?' Pierre asked pointedly. He was beginning to wish that the Germans would come and airlift the General away for good.

'Because they know what I'm up to!' came the fiery reply.

Miss Fry yawned. It was no use pretending that she was interested in General Habinger's Germans because she was not. She saw no reason to pretend to be enthralled, and thought, 'When we marry there are bound to be things that he dislikes about me.' Miss Fry liked to think, and seemed now whole-heartedly to believe, that the General would propose.

'I will tell, if you wish, what my theory is,' said Pierre. He intended to tell it to the others whether they wished to hear it or not.

General Habinger grunted with disapproval. What could this onion seller know? If there was another explanation apart from his attempted assassination, which he doubted, he was certain that he would have thought of it. The General still half believed that Pierre was a German spy.

'I believe that this servant girl was murdered,' Pierre du Bois stated, pronouncing each word irritatingly slowly as though he were addressing a class of five-year-old children.

Reverend Peters shuffled his feet nervously. 'I say, steady on,' he reprimanded. 'She wasn't a servant girl, she was a free and independent employee.' He always insisted on people's occupations being given the credit they deserved, believing with strong conviction that it induced and encouraged employees to work harder. Not that this correction was going to inspire the maid to greater efforts as she was now dead.

'As I was saying,' Pierre du Bois continued. His words had a hard tone to them, showing his disapproval at being interrupted. He had never been an admirer of the clergy, but Reverend Peters really did annoy him. 'I believe that someone came down to this kitchen while the rest of us were getting dressed, kindly bringing with them a glass of brandy in which they inserted some cyanide and gave it to the unfortunate girl who gratefully drank it.' Pierre picked up the glass from the table. 'You see? . . . the last dregs remain.'

'Oh what a dark and dastardly deed!' exclaimed a shocked Miss Fry. 'Who would do such a wicked, wicked thing?'

'I was hoping that perhaps you could tell me that, Mademoiselle Fry,' Pierre said, looking at Miss Fry with his steely grey eyes, which for a moment made her go weak at the knees until she remembered that she was already in love with General Habinger.

'Good heavens!' cried Reverend Peters. 'Surely you don't dare to insinuate that Miss Fry has anything to do with this.'

'Why, do you think that she hasn't?' Pierre asked bluntly, staring at the vicar.

'I . . . I,' started Reverend Peters, becoming flustered with confusion. He had now noticed the Frenchman's steely eyes and was momentarily distracted into thinking how attractive they were. 'Well . . . I,' he continued. 'Well when you've been in God's business as long as I have, you can't help but become a judge of character. As soon as I had the pleasure of meeting and making Miss Fry's acquaintance last night I was at once able to weigh up what sort of person she was.'

'Oh?' asked Pierre du Bois, with a sardonic smile, the

type of smile that Miss Fry so admired, though at the moment she was too preoccupied to notice. 'And what did you weigh her up to be?'

Reverend Peters coughed slightly and glanced coyly at his feet, the way people do when called upon to show off an accomplishment; they pretend to be bashful but inside are dying to get started.

'I saw Miss Fry to be a polite, respectable and intelligent woman with impeccable manners. She is a keen gardener, a careful driver and a member of her local Women's Institute. A very trustworthy, level-headed woman whose one fault is that she lacks a sense of romance and adventure.'

'How remarkable!' Miss Fry applauded. 'All correct too,' she lied. 'However do you do it?'

Reverend Peters gave a modest smile and replied, 'I suppose it's a knack of mine, just one of those strange gifts that the Lord bestows on certain individuals.'

'Like your knack of picking out poets?' asked Pierre du Bois, with an innocent expression on his face. Reverend Peters scowled and wished that he could think of a quick-witted reply.

Miss Fry, with considerable difficulty, managed to suppress a fit of hysterical laughter. How hilarious that everyone should see her as being the complete opposite to what she really was. But she had a feeling that Pierre du Bois's piercing eyes could see through her.

'By George, I think I've got it!' Reverend Peters cried. 'That woman . . . what's her name? Joan Summers. Where is she? I bet you anything that she killed the maid and now she's fled the country.'

'And gone to Germany!' General Habinger interrupted, getting into the spirit of things with schoolboy enthusiasm.

'She couldn't possibly have left the castle,' said Miss Fry. 'Look at the weather. I know that the butler and porter got out but I can't see someone so obviously beauty-conscious as Joan Summers attempting such a dangerous and cold feat.'

'At last someone with a little common sense!' Pierre said with sarcastic relief. He shot Reverend Peters and the General a look that would have turned people with thinner skins to stone. 'I suggest that we go up to Joan's room and confront her with these accusations.'

'First-rate idea!' General Habinger applauded. There was nothing like an interrogation to cheer him up; after all, as yet he hadn't had breakfast.

They left the kitchen, leaving the maid's body on the floor, and set off back the way they had come with varying degrees of enthusiasm. Miss Fry trailed along behind the men, dragging her feet along the ground. She was beginning to feel very bored and could not help wondering if anything exciting was ever going to occur at Waddington Castle. Murders now seemed to her very run of the mill.

General Habinger pushed open Joan's bedroom door without knocking. This was quite shocking since Joan could have been dressing, but perhaps that was why he had barged in.

'Hello?' called Reverend Peters cheerfully. 'Mrs Summers?'

'I don't think she's here,' Miss Fry offered, yawning slightly as she nosily inspected the contents of a handbag lying on the bed.

'I say, do you think you ought?' asked Reverend Peters.

'I don't see why not,' Miss Fry returned. 'If the bag was private it wouldn't be left lying around.' She took a lipstick out of it and tested it on the back of her hand. 'What a pretty shade,' she observed and promptly put it in her own pocket.

General Habinger, being a constructive sort of chap, was searching in all the likely places for Joan; under the bed, in the wardrobe, on the balcony and up the chimney, but to no avail. Either Joan was small enough to hide in a drawer or she was not in the room at all; the latter seemed more likely.

'You know, chaps,' said Reverend Peters, forgetting that a lady was also present, 'I don't think she's in here.' It was very easy to see how he had won the exalted position of vicar.

'Perhaps the German army airlifted her from the tower,' General Habinger said pensively. A thought struck him: 'Perhaps she wasn't even a woman!'

'I beg your pardon?' asked Miss Fry, wrinkling her forehead in confusion.

'I mean that she was a German spy dressed up as a woman,' he explained.

'Oh I hardly think so,' laughed Reverend Peters. 'She looked one hundred per cent all woman to me . . . mind you, being only a parish priest I can't proclaim myself as being worldly-wise in these matters.'

Pierre du Bois was sitting on the floor, his legs crossed, his hands in prayer, and he was humming a meditation. The others stared with puzzled interest. Having lived relatively sheltered lives none of them had ever seen a French onion seller meditate before.

'Monsieur du Bois, what are you doing?' asked Miss Fry. She was now helping herself to a coat or two of Joan's violet nail varnish and was blowing her fingers with vigour.

'He looks like an opium smoker to me,' General Habinger observed. He was trying to sound like an expert on such matters. 'Foreigners are addicted to that sort of thing,' he added as though this proved Pierre's guilt.

Pierre du Bois opened his eyes and stood up. As he did so, his pot belly almost stretched the material of his red trousers to breaking point. 'I was meditating,' he told them.

The others nodded, pretending that they knew what this meant, all too afraid of being thought stupid for not understanding.

'Contemplating?' asked Miss Fry, who had not cleaned her ears for some time, due to having no parental discipline to remind her.

'Why, Mademoiselle Fry,' said Pierre in surprised admiration. 'Yes, meditation is a form of contemplation.' Miss Fry smiled like a Cheshire cat who had just consumed a bowl of cream.

'Why were you doing it?' asked General Habinger, who was unable to restrain his curiosity. He vaguely remembered having seen a snake-charmer in India sitting in a similar position and he wondered if Pierre was doing the same thing but without a snake.

'It helps me to determine the whereabouts of Mademoiselle Summers,' explained Pierre.

'By Jove, that's a jolly good wheeze,' said Reverend Peters with admiration. 'What a party trick!'

Pierre did not reply but instead gave the vicar one of his most unfriendly glares.

'Well where is she?' asked Miss Fry.

'I believe that she is at the top of the tower,' Pierre replied with a certain amount of pride. 'It would be a natural place for anyone with a sense of adventure to go.'

'That was my suggestion! I said that!' shouted General Habinger, who did not like to have his thunder stolen, and certainly not by a foreigner.

'No you did not!'

'Yes I damn well did!'

'Monsieur, you did not!'

'Yes I did, you frog!'

'Monsieur, I challenge you to a duel!'

'Gentlemen, please!' reproved a shocked Miss Fry. She wondered why her beloved had to throw himself into these dangerous situations.

'I hate to say this, General, but you're not playing the game,' said Reverend Peters. 'Monsieur du Bois said she was in the tower whereas you said she had been airlifted off the top of the tower by the German army. That's a considerable difference.' General Habinger snorted in bad grace and gave the Frenchman one of his best scowls.

Miss Fry shot her beloved an adoring smile of sympathy which he did not even notice. How sweet he was! How brave! And how like a little boy in some ways! Miss Fry wanted to mother and cuddle him.

Pierre du Bois seemed to know by an almost animal-like instinct in which direction the tower lay, so the others resigned themselves to following docilely. They walked up the stairs past the axe with its missing twin. Pierre du Bois, of course, noticed, but he made no mention of it to the others. General Habinger briskly opened and quickly inspected the vacant bedrooms with the white-sheeted furniture.

'Look!' exclaimed Reverend Peters, who was some way ahead of the others. Miss Fry and the General ran up to see what the vicar had found. 'High-heeled shoes,' he said, pointing down at them. 'Aren't they Joan's?'

'Possibly,' said General Habinger in a noncommittal tone.

'I would say that it is extremely likely,' said Pierre with a certain lack of patience – a common characteristic among Frenchmen with steely grey eyes. 'They are hardly likely to belong to Mademoiselle Fry, are they?' He looked down at Miss Fry's stout, high-laced shoes to demonstrate his point.

'Why couldn't they belong to me?' demanded Miss Fry

hotly. No one answered. Even Pierre was unable to think of one of his sardonic replies. Miss Fry felt a pang of sadness because General Habinger had not leapt to her defence.

Chapter Eight

oan was dying; not from hunger, fatigue or thirst, but from boredom. When locked alone in a room at the top of a castle tower, there is only so much a person can do to occupy herself. She was sitting on a dusty stool that had wobbly legs and she eyed a rat nervously as it scuttled across the floor. It was bitterly cold and she could no longer prevent herself from shivering.

Joan had found a tatty exercise book and a stub of pencil and, feeling suitably inspired, had started the first chapter of her autobiography; but when the lead had snapped she had been forced to give up. She was now reduced to counting the bricks which made up the walls of her lonely prison. It was while doing this that she suddenly realized that these bricks could be her passport to freedom. Having been an avid reader of detective adventure comics, she knew that the cement that bound the bricks together was often crumbly and dry in old castle towers and the bricks could be loosened by using a nail file. Joan naturally always carried at least two metal nail files around with her, one for everyday use and the other for best. Producing the file from her pocket, she crossed the room and kneeling on the filthy floor she set to work on the bricks around the door.

She had not been at it very long, and had not yet achieved any results, when she heard a noise. She put her ear to the keyhole and listened, straining her ears. There was no doubt about it, someone was ascending the stone steps. Joan felt so frightened that she began to feel sick.

'Oh God, what shall I do?' she muttered aloud. The question was not actually directed at God, being merely rhetorical. She glanced swiftly round the room, but there was nowhere for her to hide. She was certain that the murderer, having tired of having a locked-up prisoner, now wanted to have a dead prisoner. Joan noticed a length of thick rope lying on the floor and with a shudder wondered if she was going to be hanged.

'I'm not ready to die yet!' she resolved bravely, but as the footsteps came nearer her resolution vanished and panic took hold. She jumped up, picked up the stool and took up position behind the door. The footsteps drew nearer and stopped outside the door. There was the sound of muffled voices which strengthened Joan's belief that she was dealing with a psychopath with multiple personalities. The door opened and Joan brought the stool down with a crash on to the back of a man's head. She did not see his face because her eyes were tightly shut. She kept them shut, too afraid to open them for fear of what she might find lying at her feet. Suddenly she felt fingers clasping her throat.

'You killed him! You killed him!' cried Miss Fry, shaking Joan furiously. 'You brazen hussy!' Joan tried to protest her innocence but trying to do that while being shaken by the throat was an impossible task.

'I must say that I am most shocked at your conduct, Mrs Summers,' said Reverend Peters, waving a finger reprovingly under Joan's nose. He looked as self-righteous as an angel in a religious painting.

Miss Fry finished shaking the unfortunate girl and threw herself down on to the stone floor. She picked up General Habinger's head and cradled it on her lap crying, 'Speak to me, speak to me, dearest one!'

'Well?' Reverend Peters questioned Joan. He now looked like a stern schoolmaster waiting for a small boy to own up to stealing apples. 'What have you to say for yourself?'

'I didn't mean to kill him, I didn't do it . . . I didn't, I didn't!' Joan sobbed. She started to cry uncontrollably. It was so unfair, she thought. Why was it that she always seemed to be caught red-handed at something she had not meant to do?

General Habinger opened one eye, then the other. 'He's alive! He's alive!' Miss Fry proclaimed joyously at the top of her voice.

'I could have told you that,' commented Pierre wearily. He picked up the stool and sat down on it, but the legs had been weakened from their contact with the General's head and so collapsed under the tubby Frenchman's weight, forcing him to stand like the others.

'Darling,' muttered the bleary-eyed General, as he looked up at Miss Fry. 'I thought that you were dead.' Then to everyone's surprise, not least Miss Fry's, he flung his arms around Miss Fry and pulling her down, gave her a kiss of a somewhat passionate nature.

'Please!' exclaimed Miss Fry, pulling herself away from General Habinger's embrace. Her face reddened, not with shame but with pleasure and she was not really at all angry but pretended to be for appearance's sake.

'He must be delirious,' was Reverend Peters's verdict.

'More likely brain damage!' said Pierre.

'Oh God!' cried the General, sitting up suddenly as he realized what he had done. 'Miss Fry . . . I . . . I hardly know what to say.'

99

'It's all right, I understand,' said Miss Fry, with a coy maidenly blush.

'No . . . no, you don't understand. I thought that you were . . . eh, someone else.' The General had been about to say that he had mistaken her for Mrs Williams but had refrained just in time.

Miss Fry was deliriously happy, so much so that she did not hear him tell her that the kiss had been intended for another. 'We must have no more of that sort of thing until we are married,' she stated firmly with such admirable virtue that she surprised herself. 'Why, I don't even know your first name.'

'I . . . er . . .!' spluttered a flabbergasted General.

'No, really, I want to know,' Miss Fry pressed. 'Mine's Esmerelda.'

'Percy,' came the short reply.

'Percy,' repeated Miss Fry, as though it were a really nice name like Ivanhoe or Lancelot. Miss Fry's mind was in a confused state. Her mind was whirling round and round so fast that she thought that she might faint. Her heart was pounding so fast that it felt near bursting point. 'How could you?' Miss Fry shouted angrily at Joan, suddenly remembering the blow that had been dealt to her dearest beloved. 'How could you strike this brave, handsome hero down in the prime of life?'

'I didn't, I didn't!' Joan protested. 'I swear to God that I didn't mean to hurt him; despite the fact that he made me spend a most uncomfortable night on the drawing-room sofa.'

'Then why did you hit him?' Reverend Peters asked gently. He thought it better to take the soft approach as then Joan might confide in him.

'Because she wanted to kill me,' interrupted General Habinger, who seemed to have made a full recovery. He removed his head from Miss Fry's lap thinking that his must have been the worst *faux pas* in the history of man.

'I didn't,' said Joan. She must have made that now monotonous statement at least six times since her rescue. 'At least I didn't mean to hit him. I heard you coming and I thought that it was the murderer coming to get me, so when he came in I just shut my eyes and hit him over the head with the stool as hard as I could.'

'You can say that again,' muttered the General, rubbing his sore head.

'How could you have thought that the murderer was coming to get you when you knew full well that you were the murderer?' accused Miss Fry.

'The maid is dead,' Reverend Peters informed Joan.

'Dead?' asked Joan, stunned. 'How?'

'Stop playing the innocent,' said Miss Fry fiercely, losing patience. 'You know you poisoned her.'

'Allow Mrs Summers to explain herself, please,' Pierre du Bois instructed.

A thought struck Joan, her first clever one of the day. 'How could I have killed the maid? I was locked up in this tower room.'

'She could have locked herself in,' said Miss Fry who seemed to be totally convinced of Joan's guilt.

'Damn difficult though,' mused General Habinger. 'Unless of course she had some Germans helping her.'

'Germans? What have Germans got to do with all this?' asked Joan, confused.

'Don't take any notice of him,' said Pierre. 'Just tell us how you managed to get in this pickle.'

'Well,' said Joan, sitting down on the floor, not noticing the giant furry-legged black spider sitting watching her just inches away, 'I got dressed very quickly after we parted this morning because I was determined to find my poor husband's killer.'

'Poor husband my foot!' scoffed Miss Fry. 'You wanted to divorce him.'

'It may surprise you to know that divorce and murder are just a tiny bit different, Miss Fry,' said Joan hotly. 'Though I suppose that I shouldn't expect an elderly spinster to understand marital details, should I?'

'Why you!' snorted Miss Fry, whose fingers were now itching to take hold of Joan's neck again.

'Please continue, Joan,' prompted Pierre.

'Of course,' replied Joan smiling sweetly at the French onion seller. Her heart skipped a beat and she knew that she was falling under the magnetic spell of his steely grey eyes. 'Well, as I was saying before I was interrupted, I was determined to find Edmund's killer. So first I tried to put myself into the murderer's shoes . . .' – 'That must have been easy,' Miss Fry muttered – 'so that I could decide where I would hide if I was the murderer.'

'Had you decided that it was not one of us?' asked Pierre. 'We had all assumed that it was up until now.'

'I thought about it for quite a time,' said Joan. 'But I decided that it wasn't likely and that none of you would murder Edmund just to keep your reputations as white as snow. I thought that it might be the butler and porter, as we never saw them leave, and that perhaps they hadn't left the castle and were hiding, waiting to murder us all one by one. Or I thought that it was some psychopath we didn't know who was hiding.'

'I'm surprised that you didn't look in the dungeon,' said General Habinger. 'Would have been the first place that I'd have looked. I've seen the inside of more dungeons than you've had hot dinners, young lady; during the war I was the leader of a secret army whose job was to get inside the dungeons of German castles to rescue . . .'

'Yes, yes, and very brave you were, I'm sure,' Joan said hastily, wanting to get on with her tale. 'Well, being an intelligent girl of course I thought about the dungeons but I decided that it made good sense to look up in the tower first.'

'Why?' asked Miss Fry awkwardly.

'Why what?'

'Why did it make good sense to you to look up in the tower first?'

'Because . . . well it was nearest. As it happens I went the right way because as I came up the stairs from the floor below I saw hanging on the wall a battleaxe which was identical to the one we found embedded in my husband's back, and there was a space where another axe must have hung.'

'By Zeus!' said the envious Reverend Peters, who had had a classical education as a boy. 'I would never have been clever enough to spot something as detailed as that, no not even in a decade.'

'Very smart of you,' said General Habinger, adding his grudging praise. 'It's pleasant to see a young person using her eyes. A rare occurrence in this day and age.'

Miss Fry looked cross. General Habinger, apart from his one emotional embrace, had never said anything as complimentary to her. She was jealous of Joan's youth and beauty and wished that she could possess it.

Pierre du Bois also remained silent. He twisted his moustache and pondered thoughtfully. He had of course noticed the axes clue but he had no wish to steal any of Joan's thunder. Joan had not previously struck him as being a lady of any particular intelligence but he was now very impressed with her prowess and powers of observation. For the first time he noticed just how attractive she was; almost pretty enough to be French. He wondered if she, so soon after the death of her husband, would consider having a wild and passionate affair with him . . .

'I realized that the murderer had been this way, so I looked in all of the empty bedrooms,' added Joan, enjoying the praise and anxious for more.

'Why did you abandon your high-heeled shoes?' asked Reverend Peters, who was now developing an enquiring mind.

'Just in case I had to make a speedy getaway; I can't run very fast in high heels,' Joan explained.

'I'm not surprised,' Miss Fry commented. Her voice had taken on a hard edge.

'Well,' Joan continued, ignoring Miss Fry's remark, 'when I came into this room someone suddenly locked the door on me and I've been here ever since.'

'Well I must say that you've got a jolly decent alibi,' Reverend Peters congratulated her. 'That leaves the rest of us, but which one's the killer – and who locked you in the tower?'

'It could still be another party of whom we know nothing,' persisted Joan.

'Perhaps,' said Pierre. 'But what would be the motive? Before we arrived at this castle last night none of us, apart from Joan and Edmund, and General Habinger and Mrs Williams, had been previously connected in any way. This is my first trip to England and I certainly knew no one.'

'I read a murder novel once,' Miss Fry recalled. Indeed she had once, before she had fallen under the spell of historical romances. 'It was about a wicked old man who was about to die, but before he died he wanted to take revenge on all who had wronged him during his lifetime.'

'What did he do?' asked Joan, holding her breath.

'He bought a desert island in the middle of the Pacific Ocean which was uninhabited and built a house on it . . .'

'He would have had to have been jolly quick if he was just about to die,' interrupted Reverend Peters, who always derived great enjoyment from picking out incorrect details.

Miss Fry glared ferociously at the vicar and continued: 'Once the house was completed he invited his victims there for a free holiday which they all accepted. Once there, he murdered them one by one and then he died at the end.' Miss Fry ended her tale of murder, mystery and mayhem on a note of distinct triumph. She noticed with pleasure that the others had lapsed into silence.

'Gosh!' exclaimed Joan with a gasp, summing up the general feeling. She gave an involuntary shudder. The story seemed to ring horribly true to her. 'Do you mean that you think the same thing is happening to us?'

'I do indeed,' said Miss Fry, who was quite puffed with pride since everyone was giving her their full attention, a thing that was rare in her experience.

'Do you know of any old man wicked enough to want you dead, Miss Fry?' asked the General.

'Esmerelda,' Miss Fry hurriedly corrected, thinking it best to encourage her loved one to get used to using her Christian name. 'The only wicked old man I've ever known was my father, and he's already dead.'

'Ha!' Joan pounced. 'But are you sure that he is in fact dead? I once read a book about a jealous man who pretended that he was dead to see if his wife eventually married his best friend, and when she did, he stabbed her to death.'

'Charming literature you read, dear,' murmured Miss Fry who had only ever read the one murder novel and held the opinion that everyone should read historical romance novels. She sincerely believed that novels dealing with murder and crime were a pollution to a civilized mind, and that reading such books might encourage people to copy ideas from the pages. This was Miss Fry's personal theory as to why the world was such a dangerous and wicked place. She looked carefully at Joan, as though trying to penetrate behind her eyes and read her thoughts. 'In answer to your question, there is no doubt in my mind that my father is dead. I would say that it is just about impossible to fake being dead after having fallen from a cliff.'

'We still haven't had breakfast yet,' General Habinger reminded them miserably. 'I for one cannot solve a murder on an empty stomach.'

'Of course, you must be ravenous, Percy,' gushed Miss Fry. The General's wish was now her command. 'Why don't all of you go on down to the drawing room to discuss our next move while I go and make up some sort of breakfast.'

'First rate idea . . . Esmerelda,' the General beamed gratefully.

'Shall I help you?' Joan offered.

'No, no,' Miss Fry insisted. 'Everything will be much easier if I do it by myself.'

'What about the maid's body?' Reverend Peters reminded her. 'We left it right in front of the cooker.'

'Oh don't worry about that,' said Miss Fry cheerfully. 'If it gets in the way I'll just move it over to the other side of the room.'

Chapter Nine

iss Fry, who was not the helpless female that people thought, had dragged the maid by the arms across the kitchen floor and put the body in the pantry. This was by far the best place to leave it, since Miss Fry did not want it cluttering up the kitchen floor, but neither did she wish to drag it all the way upstairs to the dining room where the other two bodies were laid out. Having performed this not-so-very-unpleasant task, she set about preparing a breakfast fit for a king, in other words for her beloved General Habinger. She could not remember what the others had ordered earlier that morning, and decided to do her own menu and if they did not like it they could starve for all she cared. At seven o'clock Joan had not wanted breakfast in any shape or form but Miss Fry was sure that having been locked in a cold, dark tower room would have given her an appetite so she prepared a meal for five – with a little extra in case her beloved wanted a second helping.

Bacon, eggs and onions, the latter generously donated by Pierre du Bois, were soon frying and while they were doing so Miss Fry prepared her special secret recipe for her famous, at least at Penton fêtes, gingerbread. The recipe was not secret just because of its extraordinarily delicious taste and aroma, but because of the incredible speed it took to make, exactly eleven and a half minutes. Miss Fry prayed that her dear heart would enjoy the gingerbread; she had never yet met a man who had not fallen under its spell and become infatuated with her. This was due to the extra-special ingredients: sunflower seeds sprinkled with dried coconut and then covered with fig syrup. It looked and tasted quite horrible until cooked with the rest of the mixture. She made plenty of the gingerbread because she knew that Pierre, Reverend Peters and Joan would be sure to want some and think her very rude if she did not allow them any. The only problem was what to do if Reverend Peters and Pierre also became infatuated with her? One never knew if Frenchmen were as forcefully passionate as they were in her historical romance novels. And what a pity that Reverend Peters was not a monk tied to vows of celibacy.

In addition to the generous cooked breakfast, Miss Fry toasted a loaf of sliced bread and put two jars of marmalade on the trolley and then made plenty of strong coffee.

'How very curious,' said Joan. She was sitting in the large comfortable armchair in which her late husband had been sitting the previous evening.

'What is?' asked Pierre with bated breath. He sat in the armchair opposite Joan so that he could be as close to her as possible without making his intentions too obvious. He was certain that he was madly in love with her.

'I've just found this behind the cushion,' said Joan waving a piece of notepaper around. 'This paper came from the notebook Edmund was using last night. You'll never guess what's written on it.'

'Slander that he was going to publish in that gutter

newspaper of his, I suppose,' said General Habinger, looking a little worried. 'Of course all that's written about myself and . . . er . . . Mrs Williams, is lies.'

'No, it's nothing like that,' Joan assured him. 'It's poetry!'

'Poetry!' the other two exclaimed in surprise.

'Yes,' Joan verified. 'Not particularly good poetry but it is poetry . . . of a sort.'

'What did I tell you?' said Reverend Peters with a broad smile on his face. 'I told you that he was that sort of man.'

'A man who writes poetry must be damn effeminate,' was General Habinger's matter-of-fact belief. 'It's like flower arranging.'

'How dare you, Monsieur!' snapped Pierre du Bois angrily, his steely grey eyes flashing like sunlight on the blade of a sword. 'I would have you know that many a man of brave deeds and courage has flower arranging as a favoured pastime.'

'Oh?' asked General Habinger, always a sceptic in such matters. Was he not a man of brave deeds and courage? Of course he was, but he had never tried his hand at flower arranging and nor did he have any intention of ever doing so.

'Myself for example,' Pierre continued in hot defence of his hobby. 'Along with taxidermy it is a hobby of skill and satisfaction. I have been elected chairman of the Parisian Fleurs six times.'

'I was telling you about Edmund's poetry,' Joan interrupted. She was now feeling annoyed. A few moments ago she had held their undivided attention but thanks to Pierre du Bois this had now slipped away.

'I apologize, please forgive me, Joan,' begged Pierre.

'Hum . . .' muttered Joan. 'As I was saying, this is undoubtedly the work of my husband.'

'Might I read it?' asked Reverend Peters. 'It would mean a great deal to me to be the reader of a dead young man's genius.'

'Well, looking at it, I can't see anything remarkable there . . .' said Joan. 'No, I'm afraid that you can't read it. Edmund was the star reporter for the newspaper and I daresay that a tribute will be written in his memory and I should be able to sell his last unread work to the editor for a considerable sum.'

'I say, steady on,' said Reverend Peters. 'Don't you think that's just a little bit mercenary?'

'Probably,' said Joan, not caring. 'But all's fair in love and war.' Now that she had said it Joan was sure that her last remark was out of place.

'Where do you suppose the butler and porter have got to?' asked Reverend Peters, more to himself than to the others.

'Heaven knows,' said Joan. She got up, walked over to the window and looked out. 'It's still snowing,' she informed everyone. 'Soft, crisp white snow, and today there's been so much red blood spilt to stain it . . .'

'They must have got through to the village,' said General Habinger with great conviction. 'If they had turned back they would have got here by now.'

'Maybe,' said Pierre. 'But it's possible they haven't got into Waddington yet. The snow's so thick it could take them hours.'

'That is if they haven't frozen into dead icicles,' said Joan flatly.

'That's right, always look on the bright side of things,' said Reverend Peters sarcastically.

'If it has to be faced, we will probably never get out of here alive,' Joan continued, regardless. Just as the others started to lapse into depression Miss Fry came in with the heavily laden breakfast trolley.

Within fifteen minutes the hungry five had finished everything. Miss Fry's scrumptious gingerbread had been awarded a large amount of praise by all, which made her feel as proud as a goose that had laid a golden egg. Joan had only sampled a little of the cake, barely more than a morsel, her excuse being that she had to watch closely what she ate for fear of putting on weight. Pierre had complimented her, saying that Joan had a perfect figure. To Miss Fry's annoyance and jealousy, General Habinger had agreed.

All three men had consumed so much gingerbread that their already ample stomachs now bulged over the tops of their trousers. Miss Fry was a little worried about the magical ingredient and whether it would have the desired effect merely on the General or on all three men.

'Well what is the next course of action?' asked Joan. 'We can't just sit here waiting to be murdered.'

Miss Fry stole over to the drinks cabinet, not caring if her beloved noticed. She poured herself two glasses of Russian vodka and gulped them both down, one after the other. She was safe, though: only Pierre noticed and he remained silent, smiling to himself.

'I suggest that we split up and search the castle from top to bottom for our as yet unseen murderer,' said General Habinger.

'Split up!' repeated Reverend Peters, mortified at the idea. 'I say, do you really think that's wise?'

'It's the only way,' said Joan. 'The castle is far too big and it would take all day to search it all together. Also, if we went around in one large group we would never find the killer; he would just move somewhere else wherever we went.'

'But if we were on our own we would be easier targets,' Reverend Peters protested.

'I really ought to do the washing up,' said Miss Fry. 'I'll

get on with doing that while the rest of you have a look around.'

'Nonsense, nonsense,' General Habinger insisted. 'Esmerelda, there is no need for you to spend the remainder of your morning at the kitchen sink washing dirty dishes. You must join the rest of us.' He thought that he was doing the gallant thing by rescuing Miss Fry from the kitchen.

'Do you have a gun, General Habinger?' Joan asked hopefully. Being an army man she assumed that he would.

'I did have, but I don't now,' General Habinger replied, looking slightly sheepish.

'What do you mean, you did have?' asked Miss Fry.

'Last night when I went to bed I put it on my bedside table, just as I always do,' General Habinger explained. 'But when I woke up this morning it had vanished into thin air.'

'By Jove, that is extraordinary!' said Reverend Peters. 'What do you suppose that means?'

'I would have thought that was blatantly obvious,' said Joan. She wondered why Reverend Peters never seemed to work out anything for himself. 'It means that last night the murderer crept into General Habinger's bedroom to steal his revolver.'

'How do you know that it was a revolver?' Pierre interrupted sharply.

'Army generals always have revolvers,' Joan answered in a matter-of-fact manner. 'The murderer stole the revolver with the intention of using it on one or all of us.'

'Golly!' gasped Reverend Peters. He sounded a little subdued.

'I really think that we ought to start our hunt in the dungeons,' said General Habinger. As he considered himself an expert in these matters he was already taking charge of the operation.

'I thought that we were going to split up,' Joan reminded him. Joan and Pierre obviously shared the General's enthusiasm and weren't in the least bit worried by the prospect of wandering the corridors alone.

'We are,' the General replied. 'But by the size of this castle I would estimate that the dungeons are likely to be nothing short of gigantic; therefore we should all split up in the dungeons.'

General Habinger, thanks to his vast army exploits, had a rough idea where the dungeons were likely to be situated: below the castle. They went down to where the kitchens were, since that seemed to be the most sensible place to start looking for an entrance. Miss Fry was more interested in finding where the wine cellar was situated.

Pierre's plump stomach was growling like an angry lion, so he helped himself to some pickled onions which he had found in the pantry. He had to move the maid's body first as it was in the way. It was now lying by the cooker where it had first started off.

'Eureka!' exclaimed Reverend Peters. Thanks to his classics lessons as a boy he knew all about Archimedes and his bath.

'Pardon?' asked Miss Fry. She had not been fortunate enough to receive a classical education and in her reading of historical romances had not come across such things.

'I've found it,' Reverend Peters translated.

'The wine cellar?' asked Miss Fry. She was developing a one-track mind.

'No, the entrance – at least I think it's the entrance,' he said, a little unsure. He was beginning to wonder if he should have avoided telling them, but it was very noticeable; they would have found it by themselves.

Pierre du Bois opened the heavy wooden door which was in the far corner of the kitchen. Behind it was darkness, so pitch-black that it was impossible to see what lay ahead.

'It doesn't look worth bothering about, does it?' said Miss Fry hopefully. The blackness was a little daunting.

'No psychopath, however mad, would hide down there,' said Reverend Peters.

'There are probably cockroaches, scorpions and spiders!' said Joan with a shudder. She hated to see such things in a zoo let alone in everyday life. 'I really think that's too dangerous for us ladies, you men go and investigate while we stay up here and keep watch.'

Reverend Peters wished, not for the first time in his life, that he had been born female. He had often longed to be a girl when he was a small boy, since his sister was never spanked whatever she did, whereas he was frequently, usually for his sister's crimes. His mother had always administered these painful punishments as his father, being the Archbishop of Canterbury, had had to keep up a good appearance.

'Do not be so ridiculous, Joan,' said Pierre. Particular emphasis was placed on her name and Joan thought that it sounded very sultry.

'Oh all right,' she said reluctantly. She was beginning to fall in love with the French onion seller. She wished that he had some other occupation, it sounded very dull to be an onion seller. She studied every feature of Pierre's face. He was, she thought, amazingly good looking. Of course his steely grey eyes were his fortune, but the rest of him was quite reasonable. She would of course have to put him on a diet to reduce the size of his somewhat round stomach, but that should not be too difficult. She would have to buy him some new clothes; someone in her position could not have a husband looking like Winnie the Pooh dressed up for a trip to France. There was his moustache too, that would definitely have to go; Joan did not like men with long, curly, black moustaches.

'Miss Fry . . . er, I mean Esmerelda, I trust that you

will not be the only one to remain behind,' said General Habinger.

'Oh, all right,' she replied grudgingly. She did not want to go, but she would do anything to please her sweetheart.

Miss Fry was feeling uncomfortable as she realized that the Reverend Peters for the past three minutes or so had had his eyes firmly fixed upon her. She could only hope that her imagination was playing tricks on her and that the effect of the gingerbread was not responsible.

'We will need a light or something,' said Pierre. 'Can anyone find a torch?'

Everyone opened various drawers and cupboards, but to no avail.

'What a shame, we can't go down without a light,' said a pleased Reverend Peters. 'And I was so looking forward to it,' he lied.

'If we go down with some candles and matches we should be all right. We'll probably find torches on the walls down there which we can light,' said General Habinger, dashing Reverend Peters's hopes.

'Splendid idea,' applauded Pierre. 'There are some candles in this cupboard . . . and there are matches here by the cooker.'

Reverend Peters moaned miserably to himself. Why was this happening to him? He was not a bad man; not a particularly good man, but not bad. He was a man of God, so why had God put him into this mess where there was so much danger and there were so many temptations? Since breakfast Reverend Peters had seen Miss Fry in a brand-new light. He had previously thought her to be the usual run-of-the-mill spinster, the type he had been used to keeping at bay in his own parish. Now she reminded him of a delicate, frail butterfly – and an immensely attractive butterfly at that.

General Habinger took it upon himself to lead the way.

He considered it his duty as an officer and a gentleman; in his opinion neither Pierre du Bois nor Reverend Peters fell into either category. Leading down from the door could now be seen, by the light from the candles, a flight of twelve stone steps. The group descended hesitantly as the steps were uneven. Once down, the door suddenly slammed shut with an ominous bang.

'Who . . . who did that?' Reverend Peters stuttered. He was frightened and did not care if the others noticed.

'I expect that it was the wind,' said Miss Fry who did not sound so sure.

'Of course it was!' said Joan scornfully. Surprisingly she was not afraid of meeting up with a dangerous murderer. To her the only dangers were the spiders, beetles and woodlice. She wondered briefly why she was not frightened, but could think of no suitable explanation.

Ahead of them was a dark and rather foreboding passageway which no one looked forward to going down. Everyone hesitated until suddenly General Habinger took a step forward.

'Look,' said the General, 'I told you there would be torches on the walls.' There were three brass holders on either side of the passage. In them were pieces of wood, one of which the General lit using the kitchen matches.

'Lead on Macduff,' Joan instructed light-heartedly. For the first time she almost wished that Edmund was alive and beside her. Despite his numerous faults, far too many to count, he had had a foolhardiness that had made him able to stare danger in the face without running away. She remembered what nice hands he had had: they had been broad, strong, tanned and slightly hairy on the backs and very comforting to hold during moments of stress like this. But Joan decided sensibly that she did not really want Edmund back; he had, after all, been a rotten husband. 'If only I could have Edmund's hands here,' she thought, 'but without the rest of him.'

They walked swiftly and silently down the passageway. A short way along, General Habinger had to light another torch from the wall.

'It's beginning to look as if no one's home,' said Reverend Peters cheerfully. He was beginning to breathe more easily. If there were no lights to be seen, surely that meant the murderer could not be down here. He was certain that no self-respecting murderer would sit in the pitch-dark waiting to see if anyone would come down to look for him. Yet he decided not to voice these thoughts in full since this seemed like the perfect opportunity for getting Miss Fry alone.

A few paces further on they passed through an archway into a large, gloomy room. It appeared to be some sort of torture chamber. The General had only one torch and this only partially lit the room, casting shadows which gave a false picture. He fumbled around looking for another torch and when he found two more he lit them both.

The torture chamber was vast, probably as large as the inside of a small village church. There were several tables on which were hideous metal masks. Miss Fry recalled a novel, *Lust in the Dust*, where one of the handsome heroes when in the Tower of London had a mask put on which had then been tightened by screws until his face had become horribly disfigured. Miss Fry picked one of the masks up, examining it closely to try and see how it worked.

'Look, a mummy!' cried Reverend Peters pointing to one of the corners of the room. He had always been interested in ancient Egyptian culture and was therefore delighted with his discovery. On closer inspection the shadowy figure turned out to be made of metal, and though it did indeed look a little like an Egyptian mummy stood upright, it was not. Reverend Peters, still hopeful that a mummified body might be inside, opened the metal casing.

'It isn't a mummy,' said Joan.

'No,' agreed Reverend Peters.

Inside the iron maiden, for that is what it was, were metal spikes. They were all over the inside and were as sharp as needles and as large as shark's teeth.

'Just think of the poor devils that have been in there,' said General Habinger. He did not mean, 'How terrible that people were actually murdered in that contraption,' but 'Golly! Just think of all the people that have died in there, isn't it exciting?'

There was surprisingly little in the chamber, considering how large it was. There were several complete suits of armour mounted on wooden stands, but they were not of such good quality as the ones on the upper floors of the castle. Joan, thinking (she appeared to be doing a lot of that lately) that perhaps the murderer was some kind of contortionist, opened the visor of one suit of armour to see if he – or she – was hiding inside. Unfortunately, doing this caused the whole suit of armour to collapse and fall apart. The helmet landed on General Habinger's foot. This made him, quite literally, hopping mad. He shouted a good number of obscenities which were quite undignified. Miss Fry, being a true lady while not at the wheel of her car, turned a deaf ear to his ungentlemanly words.

Also in the chamber were other lethal-looking devices, the only recognizable one being the rack. Pierre du Bois remembered how as a small boy he had longed to add several inches to his height, and how he had been convinced that a rack would be the answer to all his problems. He still wished that he was taller, but was now considerably wiser. Hanging on the walls were swords, axes, polearms and the like.

'This is like a murderer's larder,' observed Miss Fry. Her spine tingled at the thought of the destruction of human life these weapons could cause.

'Well, no one's in here,' said Joan. 'Shall we go on?'

'Yes, indeed,' General Habinger replied. He motioned to the others to follow him.

At the far end of the chamber was a wooden door, a door covered in sharp metal studs. Miss Fry wondered if the door had been used as an instrument of torture by pressing a man's back against it. Behind the door was a short passage and then two tunnels branching off from it.

'I suppose that we should divide up into small groups here,' said General Habinger.

'Yes,' Miss Fry agreed. She hoped that she and her beloved would be together. She also hoped that the General would try to take advantage of the situation and kiss her.

'Joan, Pierre and I will go down the right-hand tunnel and Esmerelda and Reverend Peters will go down the left,' General Habinger decided. He was now in his element, as always when giving orders.

Miss Fry looked angry for a moment but was then able to excuse her loved one's behaviour. 'Poor angel,' she thought, a soppy smile breaking out over her face. 'He must have thought that he wouldn't be able to help himself from forcing his attentions upon me and knowing my insistence on virtue decided that the only thing to do was to separate. How sweet!' Miss Fry now regretted having shown primness in their last embrace.

Reverend Peters leered with anticipation at Miss Fry, something which she could not help but notice. What was this man of God planning to do to her? Pierre du Bois, meanwhile, was wondering if he would be able to hold Joan's hand in the semi-dark tunnel without the General noticing. He did not yet know if his love for Joan was mutual, but he had few doubts: no woman had yet been able to resist the lure of his steely grey eyes.

'Come along then, Reverend Peters,' said Miss Fry with a deep breath. She was determined to keep him at bay at all costs. He was not such a terribly unattractive man but he was not a hero out of her romance novels and she had never liked dog collars. Most importantly, she was saving herself for one man and one man only. 'I must have put too much of my secret recipe in the gingerbread,' she thought, part ruefully, part gleefully; though she would never have admitted it, not even to herself, she was rather enjoying all this sudden male attention.

As the two of them made their way down the dark tunnel, Miss Fry kept on thinking that she could feel Reverend Peters's hot breath on her neck, but every time she turned round he was several paces behind her. Their only light was a candle as they had not yet come to any torches. Miss Fry wished that she had a candlestick holder as the hot wax kept dripping down on to her fingers.

'Walk beside me for God's sake, you're making me nervous,' snapped Miss Fry as she yet again thought she felt warm air on her neck.

'Of course, Miss Fry,' said Reverend Peters, having to trot along to keep up with his beloved's brisk pace.

Miss Fry looked at her wristwatch; it was twelve o'clock. The plan that they had agreed was that each party would explore their own tunnel and then meet up again in the torture chamber in one hour's time. Only an hour was allowed because then of course it would be lunch time; as every English man and woman knows, the correct time for lunch is one o'clock. Although Pierre du Bois was French he had no objection to this arrangement; this made General Habinger sincerely believe that the Frenchman must have some English ancestry, which from the General was quite an accolade.

Miss Fry was beginning to find Reverend Peters a terrible bore. 'I'm not surprised that a vampire didn't try to attack him,' she thought. 'He would have exorcised it by boring it out of existence!'

'Miss Fry . . . might . . . might I call you Esmerelda?' he asked sheepishly.

Miss Fry stared at him. She wondered what she had done wrong to be lumbered with this dull little wretch. Perhaps if she had gone to church every Sunday instead of sometimes feigning illness, she would have been pitied by the Almighty and saved from this fate worse than death. 'I suppose so,' she said bad temperedly through gritted teeth.

'Thank you . . . Esmerelda,' he gushed with childish pleasure.

Miss Fry was glad at last to come upon a torch to light, partly because it saved her momentarily from making conversation, and partly because ever since early youth it had been an ambition of hers to light a torch in the depths of a dark castle dungeon. 'Shall we proceed?' she asked. She intended to do so whether he wanted to or not.

Reverend Peters nodded, too besotted with this attractive woman to do anything else. He no longer felt afraid: somehow being with Miss Fry made him feel braver. He was not the only one to feel braver, Miss Fry did too, but then she had far less to fear. Her newly found bravado was motivated, in part at least, by her need to impress General Habinger. She had spent years dreaming about this man, so like the ones she read about, and now that she had found him she was determined to do anything to please him and cater to his every whim. Yes, she would even dye her hair with blue rinse if need be.

On they marched, Miss Fry lighting torches and leaving them in their wall brackets as they went. Suddenly, the tunnel wound round sharply to the left, so much so that they could not see what lay ahead. Reverend Peters began to feel his bravery float away. He did not like corners which he could not see round: anything could be hiding there! But seeing the determined glint in Miss Fry's eyes he did not dare offend her by voicing his doubts.

Round the bend was a row of eight cells. They were square, with no furniture and a barred door for an entrance. Miss Fry opened one of them and they both went in. They need not have bothered, since it was empty. Miss Fry saw an interesting, looking bump on one of the walls and knelt down to make a closer examination. It was as she did this that she felt a pair of clammy hands on her neck – and suddenly realized that Reverend Peters was going to kiss her at any moment. She jumped to her feet indignantly and pushed him away.

'How dare you . . . you . . .!' she cried. She had been about to swear when she suddenly remembered that she was a lady and so should endeavour to behave like one.

'I er . . . er . . .' stuttered Reverend Peters; he seemed to be doing a great deal of that lately. He hardly knew what had come over him.

Miss Fry, who was not the forgiving type, presented Reverend Peters's cheek with a resounding slap. She then ran away in the direction that they had come. 'He'll be sorry for that!' she thought violently. As she ran past each of the torches she extinguished them, so leaving the stunned Reverend Peters in the dark.

'Well, there's nothing much down here, is there?' Joan observed. She looked at her watch; it was twenty-five minutes to one. They had had no more luck than Reverend Peters and Miss Fry in their search for the elusive murderer. Their tunnel was identical to the left-hand tunnel: the same number of torches on the walls, the same number of cells at the end.

'It appears that despite your numerous exploits of daring and adventure in castle dungeons, General Habinger, you are wrong about this being the ideal haven for a murderer,' said Pierre du Bois. He was feeling – and sounded – fed up. He had previously thought General Habinger to be a bumbling old fool – now he was certain of it. What a pity he and Joan had not been given the left-hand tunnel to investigate; they would then have had a chance to be alone together.

'Can you hear something?' asked Joan, as she strained her ears to listen. They could now hear, quite distinctly, footsteps coming down the tunnel. The stone made them echo loudly. 'Who do you suppose it is?' whispered Joan, though she was not sure that she wanted to know the answer.

'There's nowhere to hide,' stated General Habinger, beginning to panic and forgetting to whisper.

'It's all right,' came a voice which belonged to the owner of the feet. 'It's only me!'

'Who's me?' asked Joan. She knew full well but was just being awkward.

'It's Esmerelda,' said the General, sighing with relief. 'What's wrong?'

Miss Fry came into view and joined them in one of the cells. 'Nothing,' she said airily, smiling brightly. 'We found some cells just like these, and Reverend Peters is still looking around them. He took rather a fancy to them because they remind him of the cells that monks sit in all day.' She had no intention of telling them that she had run away from the vicar because he had tried to kiss her; it would be so humiliating! She could see Joan smirking now, insinuating that she was a fallen woman. And what would General Habinger think? No, far better to remain silent. 'I'm sure he'll be along soon . . . eventually.'

'We may as well go back to the torture chamber,' said

Joan, yawning. She was bored. Was nothing ever going to happen?

They went back to the torture chamber, all feeling that they had suffered an anti-climax. They waited for Reverend Peters. Five minutes passed, and then another five.

'Where the hell is he?' Joan demanded. 'How long does it take to look at a row of crummy cells?'

'I'll go and get him,' sighed Miss Fry, getting up from the bench she had been sitting on. She took a candle with her; there seemed no point in lighting all the torches again.

She returned within two minutes, panting slightly as if she had run all the way back.

'Well?' asked Pierre.

'He wasn't there,' said Miss Fry. She looked puzzled. 'I wonder where he's gone?'

'He's dead, I know he is,' said Joan morbidly. Being an optimist had never been one of her redeeming characteristics.

'Whatever makes you think that, Joan?' asked Pierre. He did not like to see his new-found love so distressed.

'On that piece of paper from Edmund's notebook that I found this morning, as well as the poem, there was a sort of couplet; it read:

> "At first ten alive,
> Only two survived."

Don't you see? There were ten of us to start with and now Reverend Peters is gone there are only four of us left.'

'Oh rubbish,' said Miss Fry scornfully. 'We're not going to die. The butler and the porter will be back soon with the police and then all of our problems will be over.'

'Where is he then if he isn't dead?' Joan demanded.

'Heaven knows!' laughed Miss Fry, but nobody else laughed at her joke. Her face dropped its smile. She could not understand why, but everyone seemed to have lost their sense of humour.

Joan sat down on the edge of a bench, removing one of the torture masks as she did so. As she looked around, her eyes fell upon the iron maiden. She stared at it for a few moments then suddenly gave a little scream, clapping a hand across her mouth.

'Is anything wrong?' asked General Habinger. Joan seemed to be a very neurotic young woman, he thought. She always seemed to be making a fuss over nothing.

'He's in there, I know he is,' Joan said hysterically, pointing at the iron maiden.

'What would he be doing in there?' asked Miss Fry innocently, her eyes wide.

'Murdered, you fool!' Joan snapped at Miss Fry. Her doctor had prescribed nerve pills for her but she had forgotten to bring them with her: how she wished that she had them now. She was beginning to hate Miss Fry. She was certain that she had seen her making eyes at Pierre du Bois. 'The murderer locked him in there and he was pierced to a bloody end by those sharp spikes.'

'Steady on old girl,' said General Habinger, putting a hand on Joan's shoulder. 'You really are letting your imagination run away with you with these graphic details.'

'I know that he's in there,' Joan persisted. 'I've got a feeling that he is and I'm hardly ever wrong about such matters.'

'If you really want me to I'll open it up and look,' said the General. The thought of finding Reverend Peters's bloody remains did not worry him: it was all in a day's work for an army general.

Joan nodded and tightly shut her eyes. Miss Fry shut hers too. They heard the opening of the iron maiden's door, the sound of it being hastily shut and then a dull thud. The two women cautiously opened their eyes.

'Where's Pierre?' Joan demanded anxiously. The little Frenchman seemed to have disappeared.

'Down there,' General Habinger said, pointing down to the floor. 'He fainted. As soon as he saw the mutilated body of Reverend Peters he went green and passed out like a true coward!' General Habinger was unable to contain a giggle. This would take Pierre down a few pegs, he thought.

'Don't be horrid!' said Joan angrily. She knelt down and slapped Pierre's cheeks repeatedly with as much force as she could muster. She had once read a first-aid booklet, or rather part of one, that had stated that the best way to handle a hysterical person who had received a bad shock was to slap them hard. Pierre was not hysterical but he had received a shock, so Joan quite naturally assumed that the treatment was the same. 'You fainted yourself this morning after Mrs Williams was killed,' Joan reminded the General who just snorted in reply.

'Yes,' said Pierre, who had just come round. He pushed Joan's hands away since they were stinging his face. What strange displays of affection these English girls showed, he thought. 'And this time only one of us had the opportunity to kill him.'

Everyone looked at Miss Fry who went bright red. Was she going to be forced to reveal the dreadful overtures that Reverend Peters had made. 'I didn't do it,' she said quickly, borrowing Joan's most frequent expression.

'You were the only one who had a chance to do it Esmerelda,' said the General. 'The rest of us were together.'

Miss Fry felt her insides tremble. Even her beloved General Habinger thought her guilty. 'But I told you,' she said, 'Reverend Peters wanted to make a closer inspection of the cells, but I got bored and made my way to you after he said that he would be along in a minute or two.'

Three pairs of hostile eyes were firmly fixed upon her. Miss Fry, who was at a loss as to what to say, burst into tears. Romantic heroines always did this at moments of stress so she felt it was quite the acceptable thing to do. How could General Habinger turn against her like this?

'There's something wrong here,' mused General Habinger. 'But I'm damned if I know what it is. I wish my brain would start working.'

'I'll second that,' said Pierre.

Miss Fry continued to sob. It seemed the easiest thing to do. Much easier than trying to convince the others of her innocence.

Joan, who had been thinking the situation over, had come to a conclusion. 'I don't think that Miss Fry committed these murders, first, because I don't think she's capable . . .' – Miss Fry smiled conceitedly. She was sure that Joan thought this because of her sweet disposition and generous nature; in reality Joan thought her too stupid and too senile to be guilty – 'and second because I think that I know who did it.'

'Who?' chorused the other three. They sounded distinctly awed.

'While I was at finishing school, studying fencing, judo and karate, I met a young man who was studying to be a phonetics professor, but when we got engaged my father disinherited me and the young man no longer wanted to marry me.'

'I fail to see what this has to do with anything,' said General Habinger, uninterested in the romantic tale.

'In fact it has everything to do with it,' said Joan. 'It's obvious that he is now after me for revenge.'

'Your father or the phonetics professor?' asked Miss Fry.

'My father's dead,' replied Joan.

'Killed by the young man?' asked the General.

'No, he just died,' she replied.

'But why would he want revenge on you?' asked Pierre, feeling more and more confused. Joan now seemed to have lost the sparkling intelligence which he had been so attracted to earlier.

'I don't know,' said Joan, her theory now deflated. 'But I'm sure that he must.'

Chapter Ten

o Miss Fry's relief it was suggested by General Habinger that they all go back to the kitchen. They were all absolutely famished, but searching for dastardly murderers in castle dungeons usually does have this effect.

'Miss Fry, do be a darling,' said Joan, who always spoke in this manner when she wanted someone to do something. 'Would you be so kind as to prepare lunch? I'm starving.'

Miss Fry glared at Joan. She could not see why she had to cook for Joan and Pierre, though of course if General Habinger had asked her she would have been delighted. She disliked Joan intensely and thought that she was a hussy; even though she was not wholly sure what the word meant, it meant an insult all the same.

'Oh, please do, Esmerelda, you know how I love your cooking so,' cried General Habinger. His real intention was to get Joan alone while Miss Fry was too occupied to pester him.

'Well . . .' said Miss Fry who was easily swayed by any request that her love might make. 'All right.'

'Why do you not also make a batch of your scrumptious gingerbread?' asked Pierre du Bois, who thought that the longer Miss Fry was busy the more time he, rather than the General, might be able to spend alone with the beautiful Joan. Not only that, he really did enjoy eating Miss Fry's gingerbread.

'Yes, do,' agreed General Habinger. He had not felt the way he had after eating the last piece of gingerbread since the age of twenty-five.

'No!' said Miss Fry loudly and firmly. 'I haven't enough of the required ingredients left.' Miss Fry did not dare run the risk of using her secret recipe again. Today it did not seem to be having the desired effect: she had attracted a man she did not want and failed to attract the man that she did want. If she made the cakes again Pierre might fall in love with her this time! It was most annoying that General Habinger had not tried to indulge in any further amorous embraces with her and she did so wish that he would, though of course she could not be so unladylike as to tell him so. She was beginning to feel quite murderous towards Joan Summers as she was certain that Joan was trying to become closer to the General. 'I would rather die than see her get him,' she thought grimly. 'Well, I'm not totally helpless. I can soon stop her.'

'Why don't we go for a little walk round the castle, boys?' suggested Joan.

'There won't be time,' snapped Miss Fry.

'Yes there will,' said Pierre du Bois. 'We can go to my bedroom and I'll show you my certificates for flower arranging and taxidermy.'

Miss Fry soon found herself alone in the kitchen. She tried to suppress her annoyance as she felt that she needed the time to plot, but found her imagination running riot about what might be happening at that very moment upstairs. She felt extremely suspicious of the story about Pierre du Bois's flower arranging and taxidermy certificates. She decided to prepare lunch as quickly as possible.

After battling with an obstinate tin opener there was corned beef, cold tinned peas, tinned boiled potatoes and a tinned treacle pudding. This was ready in minutes and she was glad to be able to call the others to lunch so that she could keep an eye on them.

'By George, that was quick!' exclaimed General Habinger as he, Pierre and Joan returned. His face was flushed which immediately made Miss Fry suspicious.

Their faces fell when they saw what there was to eat, but Miss Fry looked so fierce that none of them dared to comment. Miss Fry ate her lunch with the other three but her heart was not really in it. It was rather disconcerting to have the body of the maid lying at their feet while eating lunch and she had tripped over it several times while preparing the meal. She was beginning to feel guilty over some of the bad things she had done lately, but it had become a habit that she seemed unable to break.

While the others picked at their lunch, Miss Fry stole away into the pantry to find some cooking sherry. The pantry was very dusty and, strangely, it smelt strongly of mothballs. Miss Fry did not like the pantry because many of the tins and bottles were covered with thick spiders' webs. The lunch had been dictated by what did not have to be cooked and which tins were not dirty. Miss Fry gingerly removed a bottle from one of the shelves and with her lace-edged handkerchief wiped the dust off the label. Miss Fry consumed almost a quarter of the bottle and then felt a little sick as well as guilty. She eased her conscience by telling herself that if anyone deserved a drink it was she, for having endured so much hardship all through her life. 'I wonder what the Women's Institute at Penton would think of me if they could see me now,' Miss Fry thought to herself sadly. Then she giggled as she imagined names which she was sure would have been forthcoming, such as 'the Wicked Lady', 'that Scarlet Woman' and 'the Brazen Hussy of Penton'.

The combination of sherry and these funny thoughts made Miss Fry laugh aloud. She quickly clapped her hand over her mouth; it would never do for one of the others to come and see what she was doing and find her standing giggling in a dusty pantry, clutching an open bottle of cooking sherry. Not that Miss Fry cared too much what people thought of her at the moment. Her mother was probably turning in her grave at some of the things her little Esmerelda had got up to recently, and as for Esmerelda not being deeply ashamed of her circus-gypsy ancestry, that would really have shocked her. Not only was Miss Fry not ashamed, she had often felt the calling of the Fry family trade, and had in fact considered, on several occasions, running away to central Europe to join a circus as a trapeze artiste. The only thing that had prevented her was the arthritis she occasionally suffered from. Although she had always told herself that she would be a romantic heroine eventually, she now had a nagging feeling inside that perhaps she was getting a little long in the tooth. But with characteristic optimism she had brushed these doubts aside in recent weeks to concentrate on the future.

Now that her father was dead and scattered to the four winds, she was a free woman who could at last marry a divinely handsome man. The divinely handsome man in question would of course be her beloved General Habinger. Miss Fry sighed with happiness at the thought of the forthcoming marriage. She leant against the shelves, forgetting the dangers of spiders, and sighed again. Once she and Percy were married – and that was going to happen even if she had to propose to him herself – she would make him buy a flat in central London. No more quaint little country cottages with silly names like 'Honeysuckle House' for her. 'London is the place for a young gel with a spirit for adventure like me,' she thought to herself.

London was the centre of excitement; one could buy all the best brands of alcohol there. She had always been too ashamed to buy any at Penton – what scandal! Miss Fry had such plans for them both, perhaps she and her husband would go to the theatre and nightclubs every night. She hoped so, they would dance and drink and have a thoroughly good time. One matter on which she was going to have to educate General Habinger was on ladies who drank until the small hours.

'Miss Fry,' called someone from the kitchen. 'Where are you?'

Miss Fry jumped, and felt herself go shaky inside with surprise. Suddenly worried that someone might come in, she quickly hid the sherry bottle behind some tins of peas, making a racket in the process.

'I'm coming!' she called back, in a voice that sounded a little slurred. She smoothed her hair and cleared her throat, trying to regain an aura of respectability. She went back into the kitchen not knowing that spiders' webs and dust had made a most becoming pattern on the back of her black cardigan.

'What have you been up to, Miss Fry?' asked Joan, lighting her umpteenth cigarette that day.

'Nothing,' glared Miss Fry. She thought that smoking was a most unladylike habit. 'I'm glad that I don't have any bad habits like that,' she thought smugly.

'What should we do now?' asked Joan, putting down her spoon and the remains of the cold treacle pudding. She took out her compact and caked her face with more powder.

'What is there that we can do?' asked Miss Fry, sitting down again. She poured herself a cup of coffee. 'Our only hope is that the butler and porter return soon with the police so that they can find our murderer for us. I don't suppose though that Waddington has a larger police force than one constable.' She sighed. She knew just what sort of man the village constable would be. He would be just like the one at Penton and at every other small village in England: an incompetent, blundering old fool who could not tell the difference between a gangster and a saint. It was going to be no fun having a common constable calling if there was no chance of him getting close to the murderer's identity . . . but perhaps that was just as well.

'And which of us do you suspect as being the guilty person? Or do I take it that you believe the murderer to be a person as yet unknown to us, and that he may be hiding in some dark, secret corner of the castle, Mademoiselle Fry?' asked Pierre du Bois staring at her menacingly. He had not enjoyed his lunch and so he was now in a bad mood with Miss Fry, and felt very suspicious of her. 'If she knew who I really am she would never have served up such terrible food,' he thought to himself.

'Why yes,' said Miss Fry. She did not like the way that this horrid little Frenchman was staring at her, it was almost frightening, almost as if he knew the truth about her. Steely grey eyes were all very well but his were too penetrating and unnerving for words. Could his strange behaviour be some sort of after-effect from her gingerbread? She continued, going red in the face: 'It must be a stranger to us, who else could it be? I'm sure that it was not one of you three, so there is no other explanation.'

'Isn't there?' asked Pierre, still with the same look on his face. 'Are you sure?'

'Yes I am sure,' said Miss Fry firmly, determined to quash the nasty little Frenchman's insinuations. 'I was the only one of us who could have locked poor Reverend Peters in that diabolical contraption, and since I did not, then there must be a fifth person somewhere.'

'I say,' said Joan excitedly. 'Do you mean to say, Pierre, that little Miss Fry has been doing all the killing?'

'You have had more motive than I,' snarled Miss Fry. 'You've managed to avoid getting a messy divorce after all, haven't you? I didn't have a reason for killing Edmund but you did.'

'If I remember correctly you didn't hit it off with him either,' Joan commented.

'I wasn't married to him,' Miss Fry reminded her.

'Now are you satisfied, du Bois?' asked General Habinger, who was tired of the interrogation. 'It's perfectly obvious to me at least, that Miss Fry is not the type of sadistic psychopath that we are looking for, and yet you persist in accusing her.'

Miss Fry beamed. If there had been any doubts in her mind that General Habinger loved her, they were now banished from the face of the earth. How nice it was to have a good strong man to defend her honour. She wondered if the General had any interest in fishing; what a pity that she had left her late father's collection of antique fishing rods behind at the cottage. It seemed a very long time ago that she had left Penton and suddenly thinking of the cottage brought back a flood of memories. In her mind's eye she could see Harold the goldfish's little face as she had said goodbye to him at the vicarage. For a brief moment she felt sad but cheered herself up with the thought that she had Percy as a replacement for Harold. She did not miss her father; she had lost the last shred of affection for him a little while before his death when he had wanted to use Harold for fishing bait.

'Feel free to defend Mademoiselle Fry if you wish, General,' warned Pierre. 'But let me remind you that you too are under suspicion. Do you not remember that it was your medal that was found alongside Madame Williams's corpse in the bathwater? Your story of it being a gift seemed most unconvincing.'

'What about you, Monsieur du Bois?' accused Miss Fry.

'You seem to be most unconvincing yourself. Who ever heard of an onion seller staying at an exclusive English castle hotel? I think it's you, so leave Percy alone.' Miss Fry was glad that the attention had moved away from herself but was ready to defend her beloved.

'We shall see, we shall see,' Pierre du Bois replied mysteriously. 'The guilty tend to give themselves away.'

'Oh, let's get off the subject of who is the murderer, it's getting ever so boring. What do you think we should do with Reverend Peters's body?' asked Joan, as ever being practical. She did not think that it was a good idea to leave it inside a rusty old iron maiden in the depths of a castle dungeon. 'I won't be able to sleep a wink tonight if I know that it's still down there.'

'I think that the body should be left where it is,' said Pierre. He had just been making himself unpopular with everyone and was afraid that he would be given the unpleasant task of moving it. 'The police will probably want to examine it in the surroundings where it was found,' he added to strengthen his case.

'I agree,' said General Habinger. Even though he liked to believe that such jobs were all in a day's work for a brave man like himself, he really felt the same way as his worst enemy, the strange onion seller. 'It would be one hell of a bloody job to carry out . . .'

'Don't swear,' Miss Fry interrupted automatically.

'I wasn't, Esmerelda, I was describing what sort of state the body is in,' explained the General. 'You see, the spikes from the iron maiden will have perforated the body with hundreds of holes, and if we try and move it, blood may come gushing out like water from a tap . . .'

'Don't!' cried Miss Fry, slapping a handkerchief over her mouth to prevent herself from being sick. The sight of blood did not disturb her in the least but graphic verbal accounts had always made her stomach churn. At boarding school, her chums had always get fun out of telling her bloodthirsty stories to see how quickly they could make her faint. Miss Fry hoped that the General would not want to entertain her with gory details of his wartime experiences once they were married.

'Do let's stop talking about blood,' yawned Joan. 'There are far more interesting things to talk about. Percy, dear, how do I look? I'm sure I must have bags under my eyes, I hardly slept a wink last night. A single woman can be so lonely, you know.'

'My dear, you look divine,' General Habinger replied truthfully. 'Quite lovely.'

'Oh Percy, how sweet you are,' Joan replied, with such a bewitching smile that Miss Fry went almost green with jealousy. Joan seemed to have forgiven the General for his earlier accusations. Pierre was also looking envious at the attention Joan was lavishing on the General.

'Would you like to help me with the washing up, Joan, darling?' asked Miss Fry with an unpleasant false smile.

'I only wish I could, darling,' replied Joan, with an equally unpleasant false smile. Joan looked at her watch and said with mock surprise, 'Goodness it's half past three already! Doesn't time fly when you're having fun. I must say that all this excitement and good food has made me feel terribly sleepy. If nobody has any objection I think I'll go along to my bedroom and have a snooze for a couple of hours. I really must go and have my beauty sleep; you are so lucky, Miss Fry, not having to worry about such things at your age.'

Miss Fry made a few spluttering noises, unable to get out any suitably rude replies. What a terrible woman Joan was, she thought, flirting with every man in sight just hours after her husband's murder. Miss Fry now wished that Edmund was not dead and that the clock could be turned back.

'Do you really think that's wise?' asked Pierre, his steely grey eyes looking anxiously at Joan. 'Remember that there are no locks on the doors.'

'It's terribly sweet of you to worry, but I'll be all right,' Joan reassured him, thinking how very handsome he was. 'I saw a film once that showed the heroine using the back of a chair under the door handle to secure the door.'

'Well, I'm sure you'll be all right,' smiled Miss Fry.

'Do be careful, Joan,' General Habinger warned as she got up to leave the room.

Miss Fry scowled. Why was General Habinger so concerned about Joan's safety? Did he suspect something or was he in love with her physical attributes? Esmerelda Fry was extremely jealous of Joan and did not care if she was showing it. Oh to be young and beautiful!

'There are a pair of huge, heavy brass candlesticks in my bedroom. If the murderer does get in, I'll just beat his brains in,' Joan informed them.

'What a sweetly feminine method,' Miss Fry said sarcastically. 'And so very you too!'

Joan laughed and left the room. Miss Fry's spiteful remarks did not bother her as she knew that she was beautiful and witty and that Miss Fry was a jealous old spinster. She was also enjoying the male attention that she was receiving from Pierre and the General. 'Pierre is undoubtedly the more handsome, even if a bit fat, so I may as well have a little fling with him; but Percy is obviously quite rich so I may marry him after I've finished with Pierre.' Having mapped out her future as she walked, Joan arrived at her bedroom.

Back in the kitchen there was a moment's silence.

'Just think, in a few more hours it will be nineteen thirty-seven,' commented Pierre thoughtfully.

'Yes,' said Miss Fry, and looked meaningfully at

General Habinger. 'I hope that our lives will change for the better, don't you? Oh what a romantic time the new year is. Do you know it will be exactly sixty-six years ago at five minutes to midnight that my father proposed to my mother on New Year's Eve.' This was a lie, but telling the truth had never been one of Miss Fry's redeeming qualities. 'They were such a happy couple. Oh, General Habinger, I would so love to be married!'

'Oh . . . er . . . really?' stammered the General awkwardly. He was at last beginning to realize just what Miss Fry was driving at. He tried to change the subject. 'I wonder if there is a billiard table around.'

Pierre du Bois, although he disliked the General, shot him a look of sympathy. He knew from experience that there was nothing more unpleasant than being hotly pursued by an unwanted female. 'Do you have any plans for the rest of the afternoon before we assemble for dinner?' Pierre asked Miss Fry, hoping out of the goodness of his heart to turn her attention from General Habinger.

'I thought that I might bake some cakes,' replied Miss Fry. 'I've no idea what sort are appropriate for this time of year . . .'

'Gingerbread!' chorused Pierre and Percy.

'No,' said Miss Fry with a firm smile. 'I think that hot cross buns are much safer. But what are you two going to do?'

'I thought that I would go and find the library,' said Pierre.

'Whatever for?' asked the General in amazement. He had never been inside a library in his life and never touched a book which was not on military strategy.

'Now that I am in England I intend to reread all the famous British classics,' the Frenchman replied. 'After that of France, your literature is the most prestigious in the world.'

'Oh, classics like Shakespeare, Sheridan and George Bernard Shaw?' asked Miss Fry. She had never read any of the works of these writers but she knew that it sounded jolly impressive to be able to reel off their names.

'No,' replied Pierre, who was not at all impressed by Miss Fry's ability, since he had actually read these authors. 'I mean the stories about Sherlock Holmes and that wonderful priest-detective Father Brown, not forgetting of course Agatha Christie's Hercule Poirot.'

'Oh,' said Miss Fry, who had never heard of Father Brown or Hercule Poirot. She disapproved of Sherlock Holmes who, she'd been told, was a drug addict who played the violin very badly.

'My, my, my, I do feel sleepy,' yawned General Habinger very unconvincingly; it was easy to see that he had not attended speech and drama lessons at school. 'I suppose I'll go and have a lie down with Joan . . . er . . . I don't mean with Joan . . . like Joan . . . but er . . . in my own bedroom,' he continued, stammering over his words.

Miss Fry looked shrewdly at her loved one. She had been right about Joan trying to entice him away. What a shameless woman Joan was! She wished that she was young and beautiful, as she would then be capable of competing against Joan fairly. Still she knew, so assured was she of her own attractive personality, that he would come back to her. After all it could only be a physical attraction between Joan and the General, whereas their own relationship was on a higher plane, a gift of the gods, just like the ones between hero and heroine in one of her treasured romance novels.

'Percy, wouldn't you like to stay and help me?' asked Miss Fry. She tried to give him a bewitching smile like the one that Joan Summers was so good at, but it looked a rather pained expression.

Poor General Habinger. What a pity that he wasn't a

woman as then he too could say that he needed his beauty sleep! 'Esmerelda, I'll just have a little nap for an hour and then I'll come down and help you,' General Habinger said, hoping that this might appease her.

'I might not want any help by then,' sniffed Miss Fry, pretending not to care. She was behaving like a spoilt little girl. 'I shall manage all this hard work all by my little old self. I don't mind.'

'I will help you if you wish,' offered Pierre.

'Ah! No thank you!' cried Miss Fry, who was not that desperate. 'I would rather be alone.'

'Well, I'll just pop off now,' said the General, sauntering towards the door, 'and leave you two alone together.' He went out and shut the door behind him. If only Esmerelda would leave him alone, he thought.

'And so we are alone now, Mademoiselle Esmerelda,' said Pierre du Bois in a mysterious way.

'Hum . . .' murmured Miss Fry. She did not like Pierre at all. He might be devilishly handsome but General Habinger was the only man for her. She had to get rid of Pierre. 'I thought that you were going off to the library.'

'Would you not like to come with me?' Pierre asked.

'No,' snapped Miss Fry coldly. 'I already have a book to read.'

'Very well,' said Pierre, looking at her strangely. 'I will leave you alone to get on with your work.'

Pierre du Bois left the kitchen, thinking what a strange woman Miss Fry was. He was not really going to get books from the library, he had used that as a subterfuge to snoop around the castle. Perhaps when he had finished his investigations he would go and visit Joan, he thought to himself.

General Habinger, now in his bedroom, was feeling bored. He wondered how he could get Miss Fry to leave him alone. Under normal circumstances he would have been flattered by her attentions but with all of this murder mystery he really was not in the mood; all he wanted was to get home as soon as possible. Joan was more his type of woman; perhaps if the coast was clear he would pop along and visit her later on.

Joan had tried to take a nap but, in truth, she just was not very sleepy – her good looks were going to be ruined at this rate. She got up off the bed and started to apply more nail varnish; there was, after all, nothing else to do. As she did so, she moved towards the window and looked out. It was still snowing, but not as heavily as before. Joan wiped away the condensation on the window, though before doing so she wrote with her finger 'hello' and on another pane of glass 'goodbye'. She peered out and watched two hungry robins fight over a piece of bread. Her bedroom looked out over the courtyard, though the yard was difficult to recognize due to the sheer depth of the snow. She could just make out Miss Fry's Rolls-Royce which was half-buried. In the middle of the courtyard were two irregular mounds which stood out from the rest. Joan was a little short-sighted but was too vain to wear glasses – so she could not really believe her eyes as she became ever more sure that a human leg was protruding from one of the mounds. She began to speculate about whether the butler and the porter would in fact be returning with help. She decided to tell the others about it later. Joan was feeling quite lonely and hoped that someone might come up and visit her. Even Miss Fry would do.

Time drifted slowly by that afternoon. Miss Fry felt restless and had gone for a walk round the castle before starting her baking. She felt very cross when she discovered that her favourite cameo brooch, which she always wore, had dropped off while on her wanderings. This put her in a bad mood and she kicked the foot of a heavy table which made her hop round the room in pain.

At five o'clock Miss Fry was having an enjoyable time making cakes. Part of her was quite domesticated which was strange considering the nightmares she had given her cooking and needlework teachers during her schooldays. By the time she had finished, it was a quarter past six. During this time she had consumed the rest of the bottle of cooking sherry, reasoning that as it was free she might as well take advantage of it. Miss Fry had already planned out the rest of the evening. There would be a candlelit supper and somehow she would manipulate General Habinger into proposing to her, getting him drunk if need be. Pierre du Bois would be a problem but perhaps he would take the hint and go away. Despite Pierre's good looks there was no ignoring the fact that he was an annoying little Frenchman. Miss Fry was also frightened that his steely grey eyes had penetrated her and discovered all her guilty secrets.

The door opened. 'Oh, Miss Fry, you're still here,' said General Habinger who looked as though he would like to go out again.

'Come over here, Percy,' smiled Miss Fry. She had been just about to eat the remainder of the cake mixture left in the bowl.

'Have you finished yet?' asked General Habinger, coming slowly further into the kitchen. 'Oh, good show, there's lots of cake mixture left. May I scrape the bowl?' Miss Fry nodded her head, a little grudgingly as she had wanted to eat the cake mix herself. Her heart was now pounding and she put this down to the fact that the General was near her. Her heart had always had these sensations though, so it was more likely brought on by high blood pressure.

General Habinger started to scrape out the cake

mixture, some of which got on to his moustache. Miss Fry thought that the General looked very funny with his soiled moustache but did not dare laugh as she had a feeling that he would not be very amused. Suddenly the kitchen door opened and Pierre du Bois came in, his face a rather sickening shade of green and wearing a strange expression. At first Miss Fry thought that he was green with envy because of General Habinger getting there first to scrape the bowl.

'What's wrong?' General Habinger asked, with his mouth full and now with cake mixture on his chin.

'It's Joan,' gasped Pierre. He was breathing very hard as the tubby little Frenchman was not used to running. 'She's dead!'

'Really?' asked Miss Fry uninterestedly and seemingly with little surprise. She had always known that Joan should and would come to a sticky end.

'Good heavens!' cried the General. 'How on earth did it happen and where?'

'In . . . in her bedroom,' replied Pierre du Bois, swallowing hard. He seemed to be quite distraught.

'What were you doing in her bedroom?' asked Miss Fry sharply, thinking that Pierre du Bois was a very naughty little Frenchman. 'And how did you get in? She said that she was going to secure her door with a chair before she went to sleep. And I would have thought that the library was nowhere near Joan's bedroom.'

'I just . . . er . . . popped along to . . . visit her, but the bedroom door was wide open when I got there,' Pierre told them. 'She was hanging from the clothes hook on the back of the door with a string of . . . a string around her neck.'

'Dear, dear me,' said Miss Fry, shaking her head. 'Things like this never went on when I was a girl.'

'What sort of string was round her neck?' asked General

Habinger. He had been observant enough to notice that Pierre had been hesitant on this point.

'Just a string,' said Pierre, going red. How terrible it was that someone of his reputation should find himself in an awkward situation like this.

'I find it difficult to imagine a plucky young woman like Mrs Summers being killed without putting up a fight. It would have taken a great deal of brute force to hang her up like that,' commented General Habinger. He was speedily devouring the rest of the cake mixture, as he was afraid that if he did not, the Frenchman might ask to share it with him.

'She was knocked out first,' explained Pierre, with bitter irony, 'with the very same brass candlestick she was planning to use to defend herself.'

'Ah well, that's life,' said Miss Fry. She appeared to be getting accustomed to the strange events which were occurring with ever more frequency all around, but suddenly she became serious again: 'I think that we ought to go and examine the scene of the crime to see if we can find any clues.'

'I don't think that's very necessary,' said Pierre looking worried.

'I agree with Esmerelda,' said General Habinger. 'Come along, quick march.'

Miss Fry and General Habinger made their way upstairs with enthusiasm, Pierre dawdling behind them, rather less than happy. They soon discovered why.

'So that's why you didn't want us to come up here, Monsieur du Bois!' exclaimed Miss Fry, turning on Pierre as soon as they had entered Joan's bedroom. 'The string that was used to hang Joan was your string of onions.' She was careful not to touch them with her bare hands, remembering her allergy. The only way she could handle onions she had discovered was by wearing gloves.

'So it was you who did it,' said General Habinger, glaring at Pierre du Bois. He was really rather cross as he had wanted to become a very close friend of Joan's.

'Monsieur, Mademoiselle, I really must protest my innocence,' said Pierre going an even brighter red than before. If ever his colleagues at work heard of this he would die of embarrassment! 'Please believe me. Someone stole my string of onions when I hung them on the hat stand by the main stairs before looking round the castle.'

'I've never heard of an onion thief,' said Miss Fry with a giggle. 'I'm afraid I don't believe you, Monsieur du Bois.'

'And neither do I,' said General Habinger.

Miss Fry walked over to the window. As she did so she spotted, to her horror, her lost cameo brooch. If the others saw it she would be in as much hot water as Pierre du Bois. She knocked a hair pin out of her hair and quickly bent down to pick it up, pushing the brooch up her sleeve as she did so. Miss Fry looked out of the window noticing the two mounds in the snow and wondered if anyone else had seen them.

'I think, Esmerelda, that I have just caught our murderer,' said General Habinger, typically giving himself all the credit. 'Who knows, I may get an award for bravery for this.'

'Perhaps it will be I who gets the award,' said Pierre. 'Let me remind you, General Habinger, that there is as much evidence against you as against me. Do you recall a medal of yours which just happened to be in a bathtub with your murdered friend Mrs Williams? And as for you, Mademoiselle Fry, you are not as innocent as you seem. Strange how you were the last person to see Reverend Peters alive, wasn't it?'

'I think you're absolutely hateful and quite dastardly,' said Miss Fry rudely. She wished that General Habinger would act more like a romantic hero and hit Pierre for insulting them both.

'That is quite a compliment from you,' said Pierre with a grin.

Miss Fry bridled. 'I am going down to make sure that my cakes are not burnt.' She looked at Pierre again: 'But I'm not giving you one!' She then walked out adding, 'Supper will be in the drawing room at ten thirty.'

Back in the kitchen Miss Fry began to feel happier again. She was determined that Pierre du Bois was not going to ruin her chances with General Habinger. The Frenchman worried her and she felt that he was not all that he appeared to be. Miss Fry hoped that the snow would cease and melt away sufficiently for them to be able to leave. She was already bored with Waddington Castle and her gypsy blood was bidding her to move on. Miss Fry told herself that she and General Habinger would soon be travelling on together to greener pastures. 'Oh, I'm so happy,' she cried aloud and twirled around the room humming a Cicely Courtneidge song she had heard at the cinema. It was thrilling to think that before the evening was over she would be engaged to marry her beloved Percy.

Miss Fry wondered if General Habinger would give her one of his medals as a temporary engagement gift until they were able to get a ring. She remembered jealously that he had given Mrs Williams one. Miss Fry wondered if she had fallen in love with the General at their first meeting since that would explain the curious feeling of animosity she had felt for Mrs Williams at the time, though at first she had not known why exactly.

After singing a few more songs in a loud voice which was not in tune, Miss Fry remembered that she had said that she was going to prepare supper. Her recollection of this was sparked off by the sudden realization that her cakes were burning. 'Oh damn!' said Miss Fry, her language now deteriorating even though she was not driving.

When she had battled her way through the smoke she discovered that the cakes had burnt to a cinder and were nothing more than round lumps of smelly charcoal. Miss Fry sighed. It was little accidents such as this which had resulted in her being thrown out from cookery lessons by a desperate teacher during her jolly-hockey-sticks days.

Although somewhat disheartened at her apparent lack of success, she quickly cheered up at the thought of the forthcoming proposal. Miss Fry was far too excited to prepare anything more elaborate than bread and jam, cheese on toast and some stale cakes she had found in the pantry. She took the food carefully up to the drawing room along with a pot of tea. It was a pity, she thought, that they could not eat in the comfort of the dining room but of course some of the bodies had been placed in there. 'Most inconsiderate,' Miss Fry thought to herself. One of her prime faults was that she expected everything to be done according to her own wishes.

To create a more romantic atmosphere Miss Fry lit six candles, placing them at strategic points in the room. This caused her to be rather nervous as there were now strange shadows all over the room which made her think of ghosts of people who might have reason to seek revenge on her.

There was no large table in the drawing room, so Miss Fry decided that they would sit on a large unattractive brown leather sofa, which was against one wall. Although Miss Fry would have died rather than admit it, the reason she chose the sofa rather than the chairs in the middle of the room was that as the sofa was against the wall she knew for certain that no hairy monsters or ghosts would be hiding behind it! Miss Fry was quite a coward when it came to the dark, ghosts and hairy monsters.

Deciding that she had achieved as romantic an atmosphere as she would be able to, Miss Fry left the room and called for the other two. She listened as she heard two pairs of feet thudding down the stairs. 'Oh, I hope that nasty Pierre du Bois falls and breaks his neck,' she thought violently. But she was not in luck; Pierre made it safely down the stairs without a stumble.

'You're late,' Miss Fry snapped at Pierre. 'I said that supper would be ready at ten thirty and it's now ten thirty-two. Still it's a bit much to expect a man who can hang a girl with his string of onions to be on time, isn't it?' she taunted.

Pierre smiled knowingly at her which did not make her feel any happier.

They went into the drawing room. Pierre and General Habinger, never having read a romantic novel in their lives, wondered why the room was so dark, but assumed that a light bulb must have broken. Miss Fry sat down at one end of the sofa and motioned for General Habinger to sit beside her, but to her great fury Pierre sat there instead. She felt like causing a scene but decided that it would spoil the romantic atmosphere. She also felt very uncomfortable for the big sofa seemed to sink back under their weight and her feet were unable to reach the floor. There was a feeling of tension and suspicion in the air, for at least one of the three people on the sofa was almost certainly a murderer.

'Did I tell you that tonight is the anniversary of my parents' engagement?' asked Miss Fry, trying to make conversation. The question was directed at General Habinger.

'Will they be celebrating?' asked the General, who was not really listening.

'Hardly,' giggled Miss Fry. 'They're both dead.' Miss Fry had actually felt sad at her mother's death for despite her nosiness she had been a kind lady. Miss Fry had always intended to grow up to be good and kind like her mother but she had always put it off. Now she realized that it was too late to change her wicked ways.

Virtually all the conversation was made by Miss Fry and each topic was cut off by General Habinger who seemed to be ill at ease and nervous. She made it quite plain that Pierre was not welcome to join in, and he obediently stayed largely silent. Whenever possible Miss Fry talked about romance, weddings, marital comforts and how a home occupied by two was happier than only one. 'My parents had a wonderful marriage,' she lied briskly. In reality her mother had rarely spoken to her father after having found out the truth about his circus gypsy ancestry. 'You would not believe just how happy their lives were together,' she told the poor General, who did not believe happy marriages existed.

'They didn't have to marry if they were so happy,' commented Pierre. 'Living in sin is so much more fun, don't you agree?'

Although Miss Fry had never 'lived in sin' she did privately like the idea. Of course it would not be ladylike to agree with Pierre so she forced herself to blush and said unconvincingly, 'Of course I don't agree. It's a highly immoral idea.' Although Miss Fry did not mind the idea of living in sin, she felt that she had to marry General Habinger or he would philander with women like Joan Summers and Mrs Williams. Not only that, she did not want to be talked about and ignored by people.

'Marriage is such a wonderful institution, don't you think?' she asked the General, smilingly.

'Hum . . .' murmured General Habinger, who wished Miss Fry would leave him alone. He also wished that the snow would clear so that he could go back home.

'Personally I think that marriage will become obsolete,'

said Pierre du Bois, who had a bad habit of giving his opinion when it was not wanted.

Miss Fry scowled. She was beginning to wonder what the matter was with General Habinger; he seemed to be very withdrawn. Perhaps he was tongue-tied, or shy, she thought. She excused his behaviour by deciding that it was Pierre's presence which was deterring him. Of course it was! What man would want to propose marriage to a woman in front of another man, and a common French onion seller at that. A proposal should always be performed in a room with a grand piano, wide-open French windows, flowers in a vase and a violin playing in the background. The suitor would take her in his arms, propose, and kiss her passionately upon her acceptance.

'Goodness!' Miss Fry exclaimed, glancing at her wristwatch. She tried desperately to think of an excuse to get General Habinger alone. 'My, my, it's eleven thirty. I er . . . I simply must wash the dishes! Come along Percy, you are coming along to do the drying up for me.'

'Oh, but . . .' protested General Habinger. He had just been about to argue that drying up dishes was a woman's job, but Miss Fry had already taken him by the arm. Pierre got up too, looking as if he was going to join them.

'Monsieur du Bois, why don't you go and do something useful, like jump off a cliff?' asked Miss Fry sweetly, making her wishes clear.

'Perhaps you would care to push me, Mademoiselle Fry? If I recall correctly, your father met his death on a cliff top, did he not?' hinted Pierre.

Miss Fry merely glared and led General Habinger from the room, leaving Pierre behind. To her annoyance she could hear Pierre laughing behind them.

General Habinger opened the kitchen door for Miss Fry which made her feel a little happier. She felt a little nervous, partly because she was not sure that her darling

Percy was really going to propose and partly because she thought that Pierre du Bois was getting too close to the heart of all the recent murder, mystery and mayhem. In the middle of the kitchen floor was a heavy wooden trapdoor which the General had lifted and was now examining. 'This is interesting, Esmerelda,' he said, hoping to distract her from thoughts of marriage. 'It looks like the old castle well. It must have been in use hundreds of years ago to provide water for the castle when it was under siege. It looks as if it's hundreds of feet deep.'

Miss Fry was unable to bear the suspense any longer. 'Never mind the well,' she said, taking him by the arm so that he had to turn and face her. She was no longer going to drop subtle maidenly hints. She wanted to be asked and no more beating about the bush. 'Are you going to ask me?'

'Ask what?' asked the General, who now had a horrible feeling what Miss Fry was getting at.

'When are you going to ask me to marry you?' she asked impatiently.

'My dear,' said General Habinger looking worried. 'There is something I must tell you; I'm already married.'

Miss Fry's mouth fell open in shocked surprise, her world suddenly caving in all around her. This was something she had not expected. 'But,' she stammered. 'What about you and Mrs Williams?'

'That was what is commonly known as a dirty weekend,' came the terrible reply.

'Can't you get a divorce?' asked Miss Fry.

'I don't want to,' replied General Habinger. 'My wife is a very rich woman and in an odd sort of way I am quite fond of her.'

'Then you . . . you don't love me?' she cried in amazement.

'Come, come,' said General Habinger, finding it easier

the more he told her. He smiled kindly at Miss Fry. 'I'm sure that we can meet up for odd nights and the occasional weekend.'

Miss Fry's mouth fell open again. Her knight in shining armour came crashing from his horse. She could not believe what she was hearing. Was he really suggesting what she thought he was?

'You cad! You rotten womanizer, you dastardly man!' she screamed at him. She gave him a hearty push which made the General step backwards and to Miss Fry's horror he fell into the still-open well and disappeared from sight.

'Oh no!' cried Miss Fry stepping forward to peer over the edge. After almost a minute, she heard a dull splash and realized there was no hope for the General. She closed the trapdoor, a sickening feeling in the pit of her stomach.

It had all happened so quickly that Miss Fry could hardly believe what she had done. Of course murder was not a new experience for her, but to murder someone for whom she had cared so deeply! She had not intended to kill the one great love of her life, but now that she had done so she found that she had few regrets and little sorrow. 'After all,' she thought aloud, 'he was pretty beastly to me and I'm sure that I can catch a man with more finesse and infinitely more attraction than boring old Percy.'

Miss Fry turned her mind back to the immediate situation. 'Oh lor!' she cried, reverting back to language from her schooldays in her panic. 'Pierre will never believe that I didn't do it, he's suspected me for some time . . . oh help . . . maybe I could tell him that Percy just went missing and I don't know where he is and . . .'

'There is no need for such lies between us,' came a voice, with a distinct French accent to it, from behind her. 'I have been standing behind the kitchen door throughout your little interlude with the late General Habinger and I know exactly what you have done, so do not try to wriggle out of this.'

Miss Fry turned round slowly to face Pierre. She felt stunned at having been caught red-handed and by a common French onion seller at that! She was not sorry for anything and was not going to show how frightened she felt about what might happen to her now. Surely this wasn't the end of her romantic adventure?

'Yes, yes, it was me!' she cried defiantly, and laughed in Pierre's face.

Pierre du Bois sat down at the kitchen table. 'I think that perhaps I should introduce myself in my true occupation, Mademoiselle Fry.'

'What do you mean?' asked Miss Fry. 'You're just a common French onion seller whose only redeeming features are your steely grey eyes.'

Pierre ignored Miss Fry's insults and continued with his accustomed immodesty. 'I played my role as a simple onion seller most realistically, even though I say so myself. I trained at the Comédie Française as a young man before I found my true vocation and that of course was invaluable training . . .'

Miss Fry yawned. What a bore this man was! Perhaps she did not have to worry about Pierre du Bois after all, though she had to admit that she was curious as to what his true occupation might be. Her interest was certainly caught by the startling revelation which followed.

'I am the Chief Inspector of the Paris police force,' Pierre continued. 'I was sent here to investigate a series of murders which occurred in Paris when you were there a few weeks ago. Do you deny that you did them?'

'Oh no, of course I don't deny it,' said Miss Fry, who was really quite pleased with herself and had been dying to tell someone about her escapades. 'But I did have a reason for killing them. They weren't very nice people and every single one of them insulted me, and of course I lost my temper.'

'And what about your father?' asked Pierre, who did not seem to be actually condemning her. 'I also believe that you pushed your father off the cliff.'

'Yes, I did,' admitted Miss Fry. 'But that wasn't a spur of the moment thing, you know, I had been planning that for years. He was a pretty hateful chap and did rather deserve it. I think that murdering must come from Daddy's side of the family; he killed my mother and his mother-in-law, you see, and I loved Mummy very much so of course he deserved to die.'

'Of course,' Pierre du Bois agreed. 'But why did you kill so many people here?'

'Oh, I had my reasons,' said Miss Fry darkly. She had now recovered her composure and had started to eat a piece of cheddar cheese, her favourite food. 'I did them all, you know, eight in twenty-four hours! Do you think that's some sort of record?

'Edmund was the first and what a beastly thing he was too! He laughed at me for reading historical romances, twice. I forgave him the first time but then he did it again later that night when I met him in the corridor on my way to the toilet. When he turned away I darted to the landing, grabbed the axe from the wall, and struck him in the back with it.

'As for Mrs Williams, well! The blue hair made me dislike her from the very first but that wasn't the only reason. She had a medal that Percy had given her and she showed it to me when I went to the bathroom to brush my teeth after we'd all found Edmund. I was already slightly smitten with Percy so I asked her to give it to me and when she wouldn't, I drowned her in the bathwater. That left Percy free for me. I made sure the maid found the body quite deliberately of course – if it was I who caused the body to be discovered next morning by asking for a bath to be run, I felt sure this would help to establish my innocence.

'When the butler and the porter left to fetch the police I was very upset. Fortunately, after dealing with Mrs Williams, I had taken the opportunity to creep into Percy's room to steal his gun – just in case it came in handy. I didn't much like the porter anyway, but shooting just him would only have made matters worse, so I shot both of them. I did it from my bedroom window. If they had been allowed to fetch the police it would have spoilt all my plans.

'Not long afterwards, I went down to the kitchen to see the maid and asked her to let me show off my cooking skills by preparing breakfast, but when she said no in such an unfriendly manner, I gave her a glass of brandy laced with cyanide.

'Reverend Peters fell in love with me and his death was an accident. He tried to kiss me several times when we were in one of the cells. I got awfully flustered and ran away, extinguishing all the torches as I went so leaving him in the dark. When I got to the entrance of the tunnel I thought I could not face any of you again while he was still alive, so I called to him very sweetly saying that I was sorry and that if he came out we could talk about our future lives together. I wasn't quite sure what I was going to do to him but when he came out I became cross again and I pushed him into the iron maiden without really thinking. Of course it was a bit late when I realized that it had slammed shut on him.

'By this time I was passionately in love with Percy – I mean, that horrid man, General Habinger. But Joan was behaving in such a wanton way with him that I knew she had to be got out of the way first. I'd tried to get rid of her already – after killing the maid I'd spotted Joan on the landing with the axes and followed her upstairs. I was tired enough of her flirting with all the men and thought now might be the perfect time for her to wave the world farewell – so when she disappeared into the tower I locked her in. I never expected everyone to go up there and find her. Anyway, I waited patiently until another opportunity finally arose, and when it did I strangled her, at the same time implicating you in her death. I was awfully clever about that: you had left your onions hanging on a hat stand and I decided to use them because I could prevent my allergy rash by wearing gloves.

'Lastly, as you know, came the General himself. I was a silly fool believing that he was smitten with me and his death was really an accident in a fit of rage. Temper is a thing I have never been able to control. Not that I'm sorry. After all, he was such a cad.'

Having finished her confession, Miss Fry giggled like a nervous schoolgirl. How clever she had been! It did not occur to her that she had done anything wrong for she blamed her outrageous behaviour on her inherited gypsy ancestry and a boarding-school education. 'What are you going to do with me?' she asked, wondering if Pierre was planning to arrest her. She had no intention of allowing her new-found life of murder and adventure to be taken away from her.

'Mademoiselle Fry, you are a very wicked lady,' said the French detective very gravely.

'I know,' agreed Miss Fry. 'But I can't help myself. I always wanted to be good like my mother, even though she was infamous for being nosy, but being bad is so much more fun. Life would have been incredibly boring had I remained Esmerelda Fry of Penton.'

'Being bad is a rare talent, Mademoiselle Fry, a talent

which I would say that you and I share,' said Pierre, smiling at her.

'Really?' breathed Miss Fry. She had fallen in love again! How could she have been so blind? Pierre was an Adonis! That physique; short fat hairy legs, a round tummy and those irresistible eyes!

'However, good ladies have seldom held any charms for me; they are all so very dull. But bad women are made of fire and passion,' Pierre continued.

'Oh,' murmured Miss Fry. At last a man who understood her. She had often thought that she was made of fire and passion rather than milk and honey.

There was silence between them as there came the sound of twelve chimes from the large old clock mounted on the wall. 1937 had begun.

'Mademoiselle Esmerelda. I have a proposition for you. I have saved a great deal of money from my escapades as a police inspector; criminals are very willing to deposit large sums in Swiss bank accounts in my name in order to remain at liberty. I am a very rich man and you are a very beautiful woman. What a combination! Money, brains and beauty. I like you very much and I am sure that you must be madly in love with me; what would you say to running off to South America with me to spend my money and live in sin? When we run out of money we'll go into crime and adventure.'

'Golly, gosh!' said a flabbergasted Miss Fry. She pondered for a moment. What would she do if she were a romantic heroine? A romantic heroine would go with Pierre but perhaps she should not go, she should try and reform and become a true lady. But suddenly she chose.

Miss Fry stared, her eyes wide, 'Yes, darling Pierre, I will come with you!'

Pierre du Bois took our heroine in his arms and kissed

her passionately. She knew that she had made the right decision. Was this not what she had always wanted? To live in sin with a handsome hero like one of the heroines in her romance novels. Now that she had fallen in love it was wonderful, but no surprise. After all, this was a love story and therefore it had to end happily ever after . . .

Fontana Paperbacks: Fiction

Fontana is a leading paperback publisher of fiction.
Below are some recent titles.